THE COVETED RECIPE

A Gothic Novella

ASTRIDA BARBINS-STAHNKE

ISBN: 978-1-7356948-0-1 (Paperback)
            978-1-7356948-1-8 (Hardback)

CONTENTS

PART ONE

PART TWO

To my family and friends

Acknowledgment

I wish to thank my two East German friends, who, in the early 1990s, had freely opened the windows to life behind the Iron Curtain and allowed me to evaluate the indelible impact of World War II and the Cold War: I say *danke* to Rita for sending me *Die Wahrheit über Hänsel un Gretel* and to Johanna for taking me on the trip from Berlin to Bernau. Without these two "gifts," *The Coveted Recipe* would not have happened.

Many thanks go to the Latvian Literature, Folklore and Arts Institute in Riga. From the late 1980s until the present, certain scholars of the institute have been most helpful in providing me with needed information about ancient history of witchcraft, witch hunts and trials in the Baltic region and specific phenomenon and skills associated with witches (*raganas*), werewolves, and other real or imagined beings. I learned how deep the *ragana* theme was and how its elements were embedded into modern history, politics, and the human psyche. And so, in the mid-1990s, out of all this and more study and imagination emerged my heroine Mara Liebman—perceived by some as godsend, by others as a witch—but to herself a struggling woman in a harsh world. I appreciate all who unknowingly, directly and indirectly contributed in creating her.

My thanks, of course, go to my family for their support, suggestions, and help.

Thanks likewise to the award-winning artist Sniedze Rungis for the cover design.

PART ONE

A Stranger in a Strange Town

Once upon a time, on a balmy spring night, tired and hungry, a young woman, wearing a gray rain-proof cape and carrying a large carpetbag, walked toward a light that flickered in the foreboding distance. When, at last, she saw the outline of an arch, connecting an amber torchlight to the creepy dusk, she stopped. From the protection of a thorny hedgerow, she fearfully looked at that only glimmering ray of hope as though it might go out any second, leaving her outside its illuminating halo. *But, of course, I cannot get to the gate … There is a moat—as everywhere—and, surely, the bridge is pulled up to keep strangers like me out and themselves in. Such is the order of things.* A bitter laugh escaped her parched lips, as she pulled her cape tightly around her and stepped back until she felt not only the thorns but also the fragrance of wild roses. She slid along the hedge to where a road might be —opposite the torchlight—beyond which she saw the outline of a tower.

The prison, no doubt. She shivered as she imagined what piled-up injustices, pain, and screams it housed. Suddenly, as if a watchful guard had grabbed her, a huge lilac bush stopped her, entangling her with its enticing fragrance, and held her tightly. So seduced, she let her head rest on a full moist branch, inhaling the loveliness of the May evening that, in an instant, sent her spirit soaring back to her lost garden and country from which she had been mercilessly plucked out. *Like a weed,* she remembered, and, with deliberate force, pulled herself free and stood erectly on the edge of the path made amber by the large flaming light.

Why? Her soul cried out. *Why should I look back to the place from which I escaped? Why should I remember the ugly baroness who demanded I call her Mutti but who, in turn, called me a witch because I know how to heal the sick and bake wonderful cookies? Let them die and starve! I don't care.* But she did. She loved the peasant children she had brought back to life, not only with her herbs but also with the cookies she baked and the berries and nuts she gathered in the enchanting woods of her beloved Livonia. So thinking and recalling many scenes—mixtures of good and bad—she slid down on the ground, prepared to sleep under the lilac bush that insisted on bending over her, comforting and hiding. Exhausted, she reached out a grateful hand and stroked the purple clusters as though they were wings of angels or the hem of her mother's dress. As in a dream, she vaguely remembered her little hands reaching, reaching, but hardly grasping the dress of the person who bore her before she vanished, *leaving me forever alone ... But, no!* She smiled and stroked her locket and remembered Roland, who had sworn to love her forever, no matter what. *And my old papa ... I'm not as alone as I now feel, and God will help me. Mary, our Lady of Mercy, will guide and save me because ... on earth she was a woman, and she will understand.*

Suddenly, she heard bells tinkling and sheep bleating. She tucked her locket deep inside her bosom and pulled the high collar over it so that not even one golden link would betray its secret. The sheep came closer. Dogs raced around the flock that now pushed its way—*oh, thank heavens!*—across the lowered bridge. She heard a man's voice counting the sheep and another telling the animals, in very low German, to move: "Go on! Git! You wooly fools!"

The shepherd was just ahead of her, but he did not see her. One of the dogs did and ran toward her, barking and sniffing, but she reached out her hand with half a cookie. The dog devoured it and quickly licked her hand and ran on, intent on his job. *I'm safe!* No more afraid, she crawled on all fours and crossed the bridge just before it rose up in the air. Now a dog barked a warning signal, and instantly others joined, causing a loud and fearsome racket. *Oh, Holy Mother, help me, for I don't have enough cookies to throw to the dogs!*

"Who goes there?" a frightened, angry voice called. "Answer at once or I will call the *Henker!*"

The woman straightened out, pleased to see the light now above her and the wide open gate before her. "At least I won't need to knock my fingers to the bone," she said in a quiet voice that surprised her by its note of joy, not fear. It cleared the air inside her whole being. "Make the dogs stop barking," she commanded, and, surprised, the shepherd shouted, *"Halt!"* The dogs lay down at the feet of the sheep.

"I am a traveler who seeks shelter for the night," she answered clearly. At that, a watchman stepped out of the darkness and blocked her way. He was very small and kept looking around as if afraid, as if someone were looking over his shoulder.

"Who are you?" he asked, looking up to her, holding on to his sword ready to spear the darkness.

"My name is Mara," the woman answered gently. "I come from the land of the northern sun, from the Land of Mary, and I pray for a shelter for one night."

"It's not that simple, so don't talk in riddles. We must register all who walk through our gates, so what is your real name?"

"Mara Liebman." "Where were you born?" "Livonia."

"That's not enough. It's a troublesome country, so where exactly is your birthplace?"

"Wenden. A small town. Seat of the Order of the Sword. My father is a baron in the Castle of Wenden."

"When were you born?" "March 21, 1647."

"How old are you?" "Eighteen."

"What is your occupation?" "I can bake."

"That's good," the guard said as he looked over the information he had gathered and folded up the sheet of paper. "We don't usually allow strangers in, but I'll make an exception," he said.

"Thank you. Just let me rest here with your sheep, and I shall leave before sunrise."

"No! Strict orders. No strangers allowed. Every stranger is a spy, so no strangers, no sleeping with sheep or dogs," the guard talked, now looking past Mara, looking around her at a large house with a wall running through it and lights in the windows. "This is no inn. This is the town of Fernau, a proud town of workers—weavers, spinners, brewers, bakers, to name a few of our guilds."

Mara heard the man's pride and caught quite an educated tone in his speech.

"All the craftsmen live and work here—in order. In rows. The streets have their names," he said, while another stepped out of the shadows and hit the stone walk with the handle of his sword, making the first jump.

"So what can you do?" the second asked meanly, also looking up. *The people here are very small,* Mara thought. She stood a good measure above them.

"I can bake, as I already told this gentleman," she answered and, for proof, pulled from her bag a hard-crusted bun, broke it and gave each one a half. No sooner had they tasted it than their hard faces, as if buttered, melted into broad smiling moons.

"Come," said the first. "We need a baker. The old one got the basket for burning a batch of the *Henker's* favorite ginger cookies the third time in a row." *The basket? What's that?* But Mara remembered how the Livonian servants restrained from asking questions. *Usually, the answers come by themselves,* she vaguely recalled her mother's admonition. *Māmiņa left me nothing but her wisdom, and that is worth more than gold.* Again, she reached inside her bag and gave each guard half a cookie. They put up their swords.

"Mmmm," gloated one, licking his lips and looking for more, while the other raced down the street to warn the mayor that he would soon have unexpected company.

"Why is he so excited?"

"Because you have fulfilled our wishes," the guard answered.

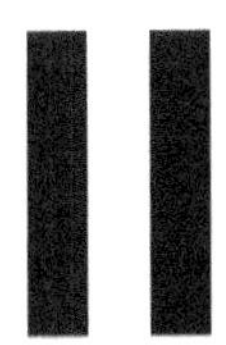

Inside The Town Walls

Mara stepped deeper into the mysterious town. The guard locked the gate. After the huge grinding key had stopped turning, he grinned and said, "You will never get away. Your cookies—and can you swear you baked them yourself?—well, they are far better than *Frau* Baker's, our famous basket case, as we say now."

Mara did not like the nervous looks of this little man who seemed so brave when he asked her all those questions, nor his assumed tone of voice, nor the pun. She saw how large the iron key was. Her blood chilled as she realized that she had fallen into a trap: a fly stuck to a flypaper. For innumerable seconds, she hung still in the yellow torchlight. The large black gate, locked and bolted, was behind her, and there was no use looking back or trying to run. She peered at the town inside the walls, seemingly asleep yet stirring, moving in the dark like an anthill in a deep forest, with a beat and life of its own. She sniffed the air and made a face. The guard, who watched her intently, said, "It comes from the *Henker's* house. He kills animals and people." The last words were whispered behind a rough palm of a cramped hand that was used to holding some hard iron weapon.

"Don't be afraid," the guard said a bit louder. "The *Henker* has a huge appetite and craves cookies, especially the ginger kind, and as long as you can bribe him with a good, fat cookie, he won't hurt you. Maybe he'll let you go, but I doubt it."

They started walking forward, quickening their pace, getting away from the wall and the imposing brick house, which, like a watchtower, observed the enclosed and free worlds. Mara found another cookie in her bag and broke it. "For your kindness and pains," she said and managed a smile. "This is another tiny sample of my art."

"I can figure that out all by myself," the guard said, licking his lips.

"Nobody can travel with a whole bakery on her back, not even a big woman like you." He became quite talkative, although he spoke under his breath, constantly glancing over his shoulder. "The old baker was ugly and mean," he went on. "But she could bake all right—that is, when she was sober. When she was drunk, she could not keep her mouth shut, bragging how she had magic powers and how she would not give out her recipes if it killed her. She bragged about being a witch. The *Henker* paid no attention to her blabbering, but when she burned a whole batch ordered for a feast at his mansion, then ..." The guard pointed to the tower and made a cutting sign with his hand across his neck.

***

They arrived at the mayor's house in the middle of town.

"Here we are!" The guard straightened his shoulders and tried to appear important. "So your name is ..."

"Mara. Mara Liebman."

"Now, tell me the truth. Where do you really come from? You didn't walk all the way from Livonia, did you?"

"No. I came from Berlin."

"Not very far," said the guard and knocked on the door importantly. "So why did you run away?"

At that moment, a rather good-looking young man opened the door.

"Good evening," said the guard, tipping his hat. "I brought you a fugitive.

This here. Her name is Maria Lieberman and—" "I am Mara Liebman," Mara corrected.

"So it's Mara Liebman and ..."

"And this is Heinrich—the mayor's son. He's our excellent carpenter. He repaired the gates through which you broke in."

"Never mind that," said Heinrich, eyeing Mara. "Where do you come from on such a night as this?"

"Well, yes, she comes from Berlin," said the guard, speaking in a hard-to- understand dialect, and gave him the paper of the information he had taken down. "For your father, the honored mayor ... she is a godsend."

Hearing the commotion, a portly man, a thin nervous woman, and two pretty, rather plump girls appeared in the open doorway. A black cat slunk about from leg to leg. Once again, the guard explained the situation and presented Mara Liebman to the mayor.

"Come in, come in!" the mayor coaxed and dismissed the guards.

"Father," Heinrich stepped up, saying, "our guard said she was sent to us by God because she claims to be a baker."

At that, the mayor became very friendly. "Welcome," he said. "You are welcome to our friendly town of Fernau, famous in the world for its excellent beer—and bread. That is, until the sad event left us hungry."

The mayor signaled his wife and daughters to set the table for *Abendbrot* and, smiling, urged the stranger to take a seat. He took his place at the head of the table and unfolded the sheet of paper the guard had given him and read it.

"Livonia, eh? ... I've been there. A troubled country—so many wars, so many small kingdoms fighting each other, not to mention werewolf and witch hunts." When Mara recoiled at that, he leaned over and stared at her, asking, "So you know about that."

"Yes, but I'm no witch."

"Of course not," Heinrich threw in. "So why did you leave?"

Mara's blood tinted her cheeks, while her hands twisted the napkin, as everybody stared at her. "You didn't come straight from Livonia and walk into our town, did you?" The mayor probed deeper. "Where did you come from, really?"

"From Berlin. Kreuzberg," she said and, taking a deep breath, went on. "It is true that two years ago, a witch hunt broke out in our part of Livonia, but that had nothing to do with me!" she asserted nervously. "You see, after I turned sixteen, my father insisted that I become more cultured and arranged for me to stay with his cousin in Berlin, but when I arrived there, *Tante* put me in the kitchen to work. Many guests came to their house, and they gave lavish parties, so I had to work hard and only saw the great Germanic culture from a fogged-up window."

"And so you escaped, right?" "Yes."

The table was filling up quickly with bowls of steaming soup, sausage, butter, and bread. Much to Mara's relief, the mayor cut into a large loaf of bread and quit asking questions. The family also sat down, enclosing Mara in a tight circle of warmth and good will. The oldest girl, as she hung up Mara's cape, admired the embroidered cuffs and collar and asked if she had done the fine work herself. When Mara nodded, she sat down next to her and boldly asked if she could teach her how to do the strange stitches. Again, Mara nodded, but the mayor's wife sent a stern look across the table that clearly said, "Beware of strangers!"

After the first course was finished and replaced with a quaint teapot and some biscuits, Mara reached into her bag and brought out some cookies, which she, smiling cautiously, put in each one's hand, telling her hosts how grateful she was for their hospitality and assuring them that she will be leaving as soon as the guards let her out. The mayor was the first to bite into the cookie, pretending not to hear what Mara had just said. He smacked his lips, looking up as if seeking an answer to prayer, and slurped his hot tea. When he turned to look for more, Mara took from her carpetbag an especially large and crisp heart-shaped spice cookie and teasingly held it out in her palm, resting her elbow on the table's edge, hoping she would bribe the mayor enough so he would break the law and let her go. Instead, as the still- alive fragrance whiffed past his nostrils, his expression hardened, and he repeated the guard's statement that once a stranger had entered the gates of Fernau, there was no way out. To avoid Mara's alarmed eyes, he focused on the cookie—its firm texture and satiny pink rose-water flavored frosting. In suspense, all eyes now turned on the glazed heart and the imposing head of the family.

"Take and eat," Mara urged and broke the cookie in five pieces. The mayor's large hand was the first to claim its share, while the girls and Heinrich reached for their portions cautiously, as if afraid of some hidden poison. Proudly, she watched the mouths savor her creation in silence, still hoping for release in the morning.

"Magnificent!" said the mayor.

"Mmmm," cooed the mayor's wife, again eyeing Mara suspiciously and then winced, as her husband smacked and licked his lips that seemed hungry for more—much more.

"*Wunderbar!*" said Heinrich and blushed.

Gratified, Mara said, "So, then, I may go in the morning."

"No, that is not so," the mayor rebuffed her. "You definitely must stay here. It's the law. Yes, yes, of course, you must stay with us and be our baker," he said, licking his lips, picking up the tiny crumbs that fell on the table. "But, you understand, I am not authorized to make any decisions by myself. We must have the approval of the town's council and, of course, the *Henker*, who is most powerful. We are all good people here, all working together, all happy to be living in a peaceful town and doing our work, as the Lord God has ordained."

"Oh," Mara injected, not letting on what she had already heard.

"Good!" The mayor called out, rising. He took a key off a hook and gave it to his son. "Take our guest to our former unfortunate baker's house." And then addressing Mara, he said that he was very proud of his son, Heinrich, who was one of the best carpenters in town, and that if anything had to be repaired in the bakery or anywhere, he would be the one to call upon. "I shall hold him responsible for watching over you until you will feel safely at home."

His hard verdict chilled Mara, especially when she realized that her showing off her cookies had condemned her instead of bribed her way to freedom. Helplessly, she looked at Heinrich, who seemed too pleased at being praised and was most eager to comply with his father's orders to guide her to her new home. As Heinrich opened the door, Mara, collecting herself, thanked *Frau* Mayor and her daughters, Johannah and Margareta, for their hospitality. Rather curtly, the *Frau* nodded and told her to get a good night's sleep because work must start early.

"And it never stops," a low, timid voice squeaked from a corner, startling Mara. Stopping, she saw a pale, curious face peek out of the darkness.

"Trudi, you be quiet!" *Frau* scolded. "Oh, what a lazy girl she is!"

Like a mouse, Trudi withdrew back into her corner and into the wool she was supposed to be spinning. Mara saw her hands tremble; she saw how red they were, but she also saw a mean tongue, full of venom, dart at her mistress's departing back. Mara wanted to comfort the girl, to say some kind words, give her a cookie, but before she could compose herself, a rough hand pulled her forward and closed the door.

"Wait!" *Frau* Mayor called from her kitchen window. "I must put together a bundle of things you'll need." Mara waited while Heinrich stared at her. Feeling uncomfortable, she wondered if she should bribe him with the small loaf of bread still hidden at the bottom of her bag and entice him to open the gate, but she was not sure if another attempt at bribing would not bring about an even worse result. Besides, *never give away your last,* she thought she heard her mother whisper. *Always leave something for a starter.*

She was grateful for the night that covered her beating heart and rising tears and, as if searching for wisdom, turned from the young man's stares to the star-splattered sky. A sliver of a moon hang beyond the dark tower like hope. When the door opened. Heinrich caught the bundle and, touching Mara's elbow ever so slightly, turned her toward the closed gate.

Heinrich The Knight

Awed and pleased like a knight on a mission, Heinrich led his beautiful *lady in distress* down Knitter Street, zigzagging up Weaver Street, avoiding the straightest way, as though hiding from the square house through which wove the high and dark stone wall.

"The stench is awful," Mara remarked bitterly. "How can you endure it?" "We must … Some people get used to it," Heinrich stammered, looking up at her and the sky apologetically, as if he, too, were one of them.

"Still, the sky is lovely." Mara tried to divert his mood, wishing that at least this young man's face would keep looking up. "The stars shine bright with hope."

"Yes," Heinrich said. "But they cannot take the putrid smell away. Nothing can. People here and around our town are so used to it that they don't even notice it. They accept it as normal, and the more they do, the more he … the more he pollutes."

Mara listened. She heard the concern, the worry, the clarity of thought and diction, and sensed that perhaps she had met an unusual youth—a secret liberator, a freedom fighter, or challenger of lazy injustice. Perhaps the boy hid in himself a man of the future and that perhaps God had actually guided her steps so that she would come to this particular town to be of some mysterious help. She pulled him at a stop in a lamplight and asked, "What is it you all want from me? What is it I must do to be free again?" She looked hard at him.

"I don't know," he said. "Time will tell." Their eyes met. She saw confusion, a childlike trust and hope, and not a trace of the cunning dishonesty of his father. She smiled. He bowed in submission.

"What does the *Henker* do?"

"He tans leather, cooks flesh, and eats people."

Mara laughed. "Eats people?"

"So they say. He is the town's executioner and is almighty. He throws the heads in the tower, but what happens to the bodies, no one knows. No one dare ask."

"But you ask. You are now talking to a stranger—you are not afraid," Mara whispered. "How is that?"

"Oh, I'm sly. I'm clever and deceitful. I'm a rebel who cradles impossible dreams and sees visions. And you—you have come to save us. You have come to bring light to this prison we live in. You are not afraid to suffer and go on living and hoping."

After such hushed exultation, what could Mara say? They walked on in silence. "But do be careful," Heinrich warned. "Once he and his wife and those awful twins—Olga and Oleg—once they turn on you, you are doomed. And it does not take much to fire their wrath. Then they charge like many- headed dragons. Therefore, watch out. If you don't, he'll cook and eat you too. So, beware—especially of the twins. They are spies, real devils. Watch out for them, and whatever you bake, don't bake doughnuts. O and O will cry to their parents that you make fun of them. Don't even make a circle with your fingers—like that." Heinrich put his thumb and forefinger together in a perfect circle. "Don't say *oh* or *o*. Try to erase the sound. I'm warning you because you are my friend."

They hurried on. The stench, like a mist, rose before them, covering the fragrance of a wonderful spring night. "We must kill it! We must end this stink," Heinrich said through tight teeth. "The time has come. You have come."

Mara eyed him alarmed. "But I am only a baker," she said.

"No, you are much more than that. Sooner or later, all will see it, and then they will call you a witch. And that will be the end."

"That's why I must get out of here. You must help me escape."

"I cannot. Not yet. You have walked into a trap, but there must be a reason. God does not send miracles for nothing," Heinrich said and looked straight into Mara's large dark eyes full of stars she herself did not feel.

IV

Herr Henker = The Executioner

They had come very close to the *Henker's* house. The stone structure eclipsed them in total darkness as it loomed over them and, it seemed, over the whole town. It stood two stories high, cleaved by the thick wall, and stretched the full length of a block. The windows cast squares of yellow light. "They're rich," Heinrich whispered under his palm, "and greedy. They entertain princes and merchants who carry our goods throughout the world. We are famous, all right—and not as badly off as others out there. That's why our people keep quiet and work. They gratefully accept compliments and feel rewarded at festivals, when my father and all the fat old masters hand out ribbons and praise everyone with big words. Then the people sing and dance and lick the hands that beat them." "Aren't you saying too much and to a stranger?"

"Could be, but there has to be a time when a man must speak his mind, if only to hear his thoughts. You are like an angel who has come down from the stars. Even your name has a saintly ring."

"I come from the *Land of Mara*, it's true. From Livonia, but don't ask me any more questions. Don't mention the name of my homeland. Let it all remain a mystery. Promise?"

"Yes."

They passed the eerie hangman's house in absolute silence.

"The house has no number, no name. It is simply *Das Henkers Haus*, but people don't say it. They are also afraid of using the word *Henker*. They are afraid of the name."

"Yet you say it."

"I'm not superstitious. I am not afraid." He spoke emphatically, completely convinced, or trying to be convincing. They were at the end of the block when Mara saw that a tower about twice as high as the house was connected to its end inside the wall by a kind of tunnel, like a long arm. Heinrich stopped and said, "One day, I *will* escape. I will go away and come back with an army that will break down the walls, open the gates, and make the people free! I will become Heinrich the Liberator!" He raised his fist at the small moon that was releasing itself from a cloud and sailing high above the tower.

"I hope your dreams come true," Mara said. Then both walked on.

***

At last, they reached a small stone house with wooden trim, which resembled all others, except that above the door hung a large painted pretzel. "This will be your new home," Heinrich said and unlocked the door and then put the key back in his pocket.

"Don't I get a key?"

"No. My father and the *Henker* keep the keys." "Oh."

"Don't say it."

"O—o—" Mara tripped, but Heinrich kept her from falling.

***

Inside, Heinrich lit a candle, and the room flickered to life. Mara saw the bed, the washstand, the stove, a long scrubbed table (*Good for rolling out dough,* she thought) with some chairs and a wardrobe. "Nice," she nodded, but when she opened the wardrobe, she almost fell backward. Long gray skirts and white aprons hung ghostlike on large iron knobs. On a shelf hung a row of baker's hats—starched and ready. Mara took one down and put it on her head, saying, "So I must take over where she left off." But Heinrich pulled the headdress off, exclaiming, "No, no! Don't!" He yanked the old baker's belongings out and rolled them in a bundle. "I didn't know this was still full of her, the wretched woman. I'll burn everything so she won't haunt you."

Chilled, Mara said that she was not afraid, that she did not believe in ghosts and was not superstitious. She added that she didn't believe in witches either, and Heinrich said, "*Good,*" because, he explained, the belief was much stronger all around than an army of witches could ever be. "There has to come another crusade," he said, but Mara stepped into the next room, stooping so she would not hit her head.

"This is the bakery," Heinrich explained, holding the candle high. "Here is the oven. Here, the workbench. There, the display window, now shuttered and dirty."

Mara took a deep breath and then examined the huge stone oven. "A person could fit in there," she said, peering inside. Suddenly, she felt a push and heard a mean laugh, as she was being pulled back. "Beware you don't!" Heinrich said, holding her tightly, saying gently, "Don't be afraid of me. I'll be your friend and protector, but never, ever turn your back to Oleg." Then after setting the candle down, he knelt on one knee, took her hand, and pressed his forehead against it. "I swear I will always protect you," he said. She put her hand on his shoulder and thanked him. He rose rather awkwardly and stood facing her, their eyes meeting.

"Well, my knight, so when may I leave?" she asked. "Only God knows," he answered, shaking his head.

Unsatisfied, Mara glanced around the room. She saw that the bins were full of flour and the shelves full of spices. The ginger hung in the air, overpowering the cardamom and anise and all else. She saw plenty of wood next to the oven. "I will rise early, bake some cookies, and then you'll show me the way out. I must get away!"

"No! You must not leave this town yet, and, besides, they will not let you. Not even my father can help. It is the *Henker* who rules here, and he has a passion for ginger cookies, and so do Olga and Oleg. His wife, though, is allergic to ginger and hates it. But that doesn't matter. The *Henker* orders the cookies day or night, and if you don't bake, if you don't make him think he gets the best in the world, he will order you to the tower—the way he did the old baker."

"Then I am trapped."

"Yes. Same as I. Same as all of us, and, like all of us, in time, you will learn to accept and even like the wall. You will learn not to see it, not to look up at the tower, nor try to gaze over the wall with eyes full of visions and longing. You will learn to look inward and feel safe because a wall of protection encloses you."

Mara stared at him. She stared at the lips that moved, making sounds— words, concepts that terrified her and contradicted each other. He seemed all mixed up so that she wondered if she had not talked too freely too quickly, too trustingly. She watched the flame of the candle shooting up and flickering about, getting long and unruly. "So I'm trapped," she repeated thoughtfully, "and dependent only on you, o—ahh," she sighed. "Please go. I'm very tired."

"I'll come for you in the morning. You must be presented to the town's council, which always has the last word."

Mara caught the irony of the pun but let it pass. "It's only a procedure," Heinrich assured her. "A formality. You understand? You are an intruder, a foreigner, maybe a …"

"Yes, I understand," Mara said and pushed the bundle of the former baker's clothes at him. She opened the door. "Good night," she said hastelly.

"But are you a witch or a saint?" he asked, standing still, looking up bewildered, the bundle hanging from his arm.

"I am neither. I am only a woman, as I told you, from the distant, and to you strange, land of Livonia, the land your Crusaders vanquished hundreds of years ago."

"Are you very afraid?"

"Yes—but no. No. Because I shall try to do only good and so will win the love of your people and, perhaps, even the respect of this *Henker,* who is only a man, after all. Besides, don't I have your trust and loyalty, or are you the one who is afraid?" She saw how childlike his face was, smooth with some blemishes. Veiling his upper lip edged a black downy mustache. A face in transition, she thought and said, "Go on home."

But he still stood, looking up. "You are so beautiful, and I feel a strange power in your presence."

"I thank you. But such beauty as I have is a gift of my mother, and what power I may have comes from my land … from the beloved forests and meadows I had to leave. That hard earth was my school and my church. My father still lives there," she said musing, looking in the distant heavens. "And he waits for me." She touched the locket hiding inside her dress and remembered her beloved Roland, while hardly hearing Heinrich's heavily accented speech.

"Perhaps what I feel is the strength of the land you have brought with you. It will also make me strong, and together we will help bring down this evil empire." He spoke as to a shrine. Mara, becoming impatient and cold, pulled her cape around her and listened, looking down. He seemed foolish, almost a nuisance, but he was the only friend she had in this strange town.

"How old are you, if I may ask?" "Sixteen, soon to be seventeen."

"It's a nice age," she smiled, saying, "Good night, my gentle knight." "Good night, my lady."

***

She stood, framed by the open door, and watched Heinrich disappear around a corner. She tried not to smell the stench of burning leather and breathed deeply the fragrance of what could have been a most unusual evening.

"A ghost! A ghost! The witch isn't dead!"

The screams of young voices shredded the darkness. Mara hid herself inside and barricaded the door, while the evening bells of the church rang in the midnight hour. She forced herself to make a bed, undress, and lie down. But, of course, she could not sleep. Looking at the low ceiling, she remembered and memorized all that had happened on her long flight from Livonia and the twists and turns of her journey that had brought her to this strangely frightening yet almost enchanting little town. She tried to understand Heinrich and his romantic vision of her and the loyalty he swore. *A strange young man,* she smiled, truly grateful that there was someone she could trust—if not completely, then enough to feel quite protected. Thinking over her new and strange circumstances, she was startled when she heard someone locking her door and banging on the shutters. She sat up and held her breath. *Oh, of course! Olga and Oleg* ... They had come to lock the door of the bakery and had seen her standing in the doorway and assumed she was the ghost of the tortured woman who had baked and burned their cookies. Perhaps more frightened than she, they had run away to the safety of their ghastly house. Slowly, still listening, she laid her head on the thin, musty pillow that faintly smelled of the poor dead woman and closed her eyes. She slept well.

V

Happy Village

Mara awoke with the singing and trilling birds. She opened her small window. The air smelled sweet, though tinged with the hovering stench. The streets and houses, still veiled in dawn, reminded her of the painting on her father's castle wall back home: *A Happy Village*. Now, she felt she was the absent form of that painting. *I could be merely a stroke of brushes, a fusion of color... And does my charming prince Roland think of me?* She opened the locket and kissed the lock of his golden hair. *I will never forget you, and I will come back to you. Only be faithful and wait. I love you so!*

Suddenly, as a starling sang his morning call, she felt she had, in truth, come to a most enchanting place—an isle—a jewel box set in a lovely valley. *I am the lady in distress, and I have a knight who adores me! I shall do magic and dangerous deeds, knowing the knight will be ever faithful and protect me. And then, together, we will defeat all evil, and I shall return home to my loved ones, free and happy. It would take some time, some adventure, but it will happen...* Not entirely convinced, she looked at the wall and saw how rigidly it ran all around the town, as if protecting it from wars and uprisings and how the people, one by one coming out of their houses, dressed in simple garb, did not seem to notice it, as they went about their businesses and their assigned labors.

A Happy Village ... Indeed.

VI

Before The Town Council

The terror of the night evaporated as quickly as the dark clouds and sheer mist above the tower. She thanked God for bringing her safely this far and went to work. Before the clock struck noon, Mara had baked a batch of cookies that were so wonderfully fragrant that curious people gathered around her door and windows but then rushed away to go and tell others. When, at last, Heinrich appeared, all dressed up and walking through the crowd like a true knight, Mara came out, wearing her gray traveling suit and carrying a large basket covered with a shining linen napkin—a small keepsake from home. The crowd opened up to let the eager knight escort his lady to the *Rathaus*.

***

Inside the town hall, all the important people had gathered. The mayor properly presented Mara to the priest and the *Henker*: "This woman arrived at our gate late last night and humbly asked for shelter. Her name is Mara Liebman, who was born in our Livonian province and came to Berlin to work. However, because of uncertain circumstances, she left Berlin and sought refuge in our town." He spoke on, embellishing his story as his imagination and greed dictated, lying that she wanted to be a part of this town and work as a baker. When Mara tried to object and say that she wanted out, the mayor put her down with a hard look and, appealing to the *Henker,* reiterated the fact that Fernau needed a baker. After much deliberation, her cookies were passed around. The men tasted them, and then they ate and tasted more and more. There was a most noisy smacking of lips and such noises that are made by closed, full mouths afraid to let the crumbs drop.

At last, the *Henker* stood up and ordered the whole basket to be set before him. The huge man ate the cookies, devouring them as though he had not seen food for days. Mara saw how the others stared at this man, most richly dressed yet having the manners of a beast. She saw suspended fear, anxiety, and impatience. She clenched her fists, hoping that this *Henker* would not like the cookies and would throw her out, but all in vain. She saw the mayor cast worried glances at her, telling her with his eyes to keep still. She saw that they were at cross purposes, each pulling his/her own way. He winked a tiny, sparkling wink, but she rebuked him with a stern look just as she heard the *Henker* say, "She can stay. She *must* stay!"

Hearing that, Mara's blood seemed to drain from her as all hope of freedom evaporated. The *Henker*, in full satisfaction, fell back into his huge chair and looked at Mara as if she, too, were some dish prepared only for him. "See," he gloated, "didn't we do right? Isn't she better than the other?" The council nodded as with one twist of a string.

The *Henker* motioned with his fat finger for Mara to come closer. She did. For a moment, she stood facing the monster and then quickly pulled her basket away. "More," the *Henker* growled, snatching at the basket. "Give me more!"

"No!" Mara said, quickly assessing her situation and standing tall. "You have had enough. There are women and children outside. They, too, should have a taste. I want to be accepted by all the people. I don't want them to call me a ghost and run from me, but honor and trust me." She glanced at Heinrich, who stood close to the door, ready to bolt. She smiled, scanning the whole room, and then, resting her eyes on the powerful three, said, "If all of you have conspired to keep me inside these walls, then at least you must let me be free and freely work for you as best I can. I shall only want to do the people and this town good. I hope we all shall stop being afraid."

Before the *Henker* could speak, aghast as he was at being contradicted and overpowered by a woman's words, the priest rose to dismiss the meeting. But Mara spoke up. "One more question, if you please."

"Yes," they all said with one cracked voice. "What will you pay me?"

"Pay?" the *Henker* yelled. "Pay?"

"Yes, pay," she said clearly with a touch of an accent. "Isn't this town known the world over for its justice and riches?"

"So it is," said the mayor, "and its beer."

The treasurer quickly promised one *thaler* for a day's work and a bonus gift for the holidays. The priest nodded, but the *Henker* growled. "A conspiracy!" He slapped the table and shouted, "Treason!" But the priest said that a laborer was worthy of his and even *her* wages and said the blessing and the benediction. The mayor called the meeting adjourned.

Heinrich escorted Mara out. He led her through the curious crowd, while she tossed out the remaining cookies to the many outstretched hands. When she was safely in her house, she opened the window and, leaning out, gave a cookie to all those who reached up. She gave until she had nothing left, and then she closed the window and rested. Heinrich stood by at a distance. When all the people had gone away, the *Henker* came and pounded on the door, yelling, "More, give me more, you witch!"

Mara leaned over and above him and said, "No. Besides, I have nothing more to give. And please do not call me names."

The *Henker* grit his teeth. "How dare you mouth back to me! How dare you contradict me! No one does. No one ever does. You'll hang for this! Don't you know that I am all powerful here and what I say goes? Hasn't that milk- faced boy told you about our famous tower?"

"No."

"Well, then, let me do the honors. See, inside there, at the bottom are the bones of the dead—the rebellious, stupid, disobedient dead. The latest was the baker in whose bed you sleep. Here's the procedure: I order the wretches to be put in a basket that hangs from the ceiling. Then we lower them down and let them dangle in the dark for several days, depending how my time goes. They dangle over the bones and skulls of others. We never clean the place because, then, the effect would be lost. So … follow me so far?"

The man grinned, his brown teeth showing, his head moving closer to hers. Mara pulled herself back, thinking, *He stinks like a carcass.* "Well, so they dangle—their last swing, so to speak—and then we pull them up and put them in a room that's high up and closed but big enough for the priest to sit with his sinner and hear the last confession. I give the church what it asks, you know, but I myself believe nothing—neither God nor devil—but only my two hands. Then the absolved is turned over to me, and I finish him or her off

—quick and easy—like that." He cut his hand across his neck. Mara shut her eyes.

"Clear?"

"Very."

The monster spit and cursed. "Now, give me my cookies, and you have nothing to fear."

"I am not afraid of you."

She watched him salivate like a mad dog. *Always be kind to mad dogs.* She said, "I don't mean to offend you, kind sir. Indeed, I wish to thank you for letting me stay here and work. I shall bake more cookies. You have tasted only a small sample of my art. I have a recipe for each day of the year and for all the holidays. You will be pleased, but you must not overeat. It's not healthy. Too much sugar and spice is bad for your liver."

"Quiet!" he shouted, but his voice cracked, and, sniveling, he shuffled away.

He clearly suffers from gout. Mara saw and closed the door. She leaned against the cold, strange door, tears of rage and terror running down her cheeks. *Again,* she cried in a whisper only God would hear. *Again, I'll have to struggle and fight. Why? Why, why, oh, God, and all ye saints? Can't you yourselves fight the evils of this world? Is all the fire and brimstone in your high storehouses gone? Must I fight only with my hands? Or with my cookies? Oh, why didst thou give me the gift of baking, and why didst thou put glutenous, bloodthirsty men and jealous women in my path? Why was I born, oh Lord Almighty?* She knelt and crossed herself. *Please forgive me my trespasses ... Give us this day our daily bread and lead us not into temptation, for thine is the kingdom, and the power, and the glory forever and ever. Amen.*

She rose from the dusty floor as from a grave. *Not by works alone are ye saved, but by faith ...* She had heard that spoken from the pulpits many times. *But for me it will be the works, because I am a woman* went through her mind, as if a little devil played a fiddle inside her head. Not to be misunderstood by the Almighty, she added, *All right. I'll bake all I can and believe, believe that thou wilt save me, if it be thy will. Only give me love, not fear and hate. Inspire my imagination and bless these my two hands. In the name of Christ and his Mother and all the saints, dear God, I pray for that … Amen. Amen.*

She tied an apron around her and started working.

VII

Mara The Baker

In Fernau, daily life, however rattled by the arrival of the stranger, soon fell in the groove of normal routine: the spinners spun, the weavers wove, the brewers brewed, the butchers butchered, the mayor governed, the treasurer counted the money, and the Henker ruled over all. Mara's shelves were filled regularly with spices from foreign merchants and staple necessities from surrounding peasants. She only had to ask, and all was given—delivered by young men in colorful costumes.

Mara baked. She baked every day throughout the whole year. She baked loaves of brown, white, and gray bread. She baked sweet, plain, and sourdough. She baked all kinds of buns—hot crossed and with surprises in the middle; she formed pretzels of all sizes and gave them to the children who, full of curiosity, passed by her window every day. And, of course, she baked cookies. She baked countless varieties, shapes, and flavors. On holy and saint's days and folk holidays and on Christmas, Easter, and Whitsunday, she baked scrumptious wonders as though they were sprinkled with special blessing from heaven. When she carried her samples to the altar, the priest blessed them with drops of holy water and ate them, praising God and the hands he used. On those special days, she dressed up in her white Livonian costume she had ordered the craftsmen of Fernau to create. She drew the designs and patterns as authentically as she remembered. However, the longer she stayed in Fernau, the more her early life in Livonia seemed to fade away like a dream. Yet she clung to the foggy dream. In solitude, she stroked her locket and sang songs and prayed in the ancient language so she would not forget anything and anybody. Publicly, she tried to conform, but no matter what, to the natives, she was and would always remain an outsider, a foreigner, and always be suspect of something or other. Lately, she was aware that the townspeople gossiped about her and Heinrich, expecting that they marry, for what other reason was there for him to be always at her side? But she let all gossip pass her by. Her pastries excited her far more than all Heinrich's smiles and frowns.

The most favored cookies were her *Leben Kuchen*—cakes/cookies of life. She had discovered the cookies right before Christmas in a *Kondetorai* in Berlin, but when she asked for the recipe, the owner chased her out the door. Then she tried to guess the ingredients, experimenting with spices and proportions until she thought she had a perfect match. She was satisfied when, at the Christmas Eve soiree at the uncle's mansion, a group of older men and ladies tasted them and smacked their lips, nodding pleasantly, and asked Mara what she called them.

"*Leben Kuchen*," she said.

"You mean *Lebkuchen?*" corrected one of the women. "Yes, I suppose so."

"Good, very good," said a man.

"But not the same ... no, not the same," a woman added, chewing slowly. "Something's missing, some peculiar ingredient."

"Same as what?" Mara asked. "What's missing?" "That, my dear, no one knows. It was her secret." "Whose?"

"Why, Katharina Schraderin's, the famous *Bakkerhexe's*, as she was well known."

"*Hexe?*" Mara could barely whisper the question.

"Yes," joined in another man, "that's what they said she was. A witch. There was a hearing of sorts, and she was let go and supposedly went back to work, but then, no one knows what happened to her. She disappeared, vanished from sight, which is a common practice among witches."

"And the recipe flew away with her," added another. "What you can buy around here is close, but not it. Like yours. They're good, though, but not as good as hers, but keep trying. Make a name for yourself. Anyway, the young people never tasted the real thing and don't know the difference ... People forget."

"Time covers and buries everything … Our graveyards are closed books," a philosopher added.

"Maybe someday, someone will open the closed book and discover the secret and the truth about what really happened to the *Bakkerhexe*," said another as he drank his wine.

"So it's all a mystery?" Mara injected. "Yes. To be sure. So 'tis."

***

Since that Christmas party a year ago, Mara had tried to guess the secret ingredient but had no luck. Still, for lack of no better name, she stuck with *Leben Kuchen—life cakes, cakes of life* … She liked that. The cookies had a kick. They seemed to wake up dormant taste buds, add a bit of spice to life. She was pleased.

The main ingredient was ginger, which she learned to balance out with molasses and other spices. Everyone liked them and ate them slowly, allowing the taste buds to open up to the mystery of true culinary art given only to certain people. The Fernauers did not criticize Mara's cookies as the high-society Berlin people had but bought them out quickly, so that she could hardly keep up with their demand. The *Henker* surely liked them, which mattered the most.

Actually, Mara preferred a similar spice cookie the Livonian women baked for Christmas known as *piparkūkas*, pepper cookies, because the recipe called for a pinch of white pepper and special salt that came from the horns of oxen. As she rolled out the molasses-tinted dark dough, she remembered the ways of those women who could not read or write but knew countless ways of baking and cooking. She also remembered how, when they worked, they told tales and sang songs that had been passed down the ages and which they, too, passed on. In such a way, the wisdom of ages went on and on in a never- interrupted chain. Mara sensed that she was a link in that chain, no matter what, and, therefore, she baked those cookies and worked the way she remembered the women working from sunrise until sunset. She marveled how those women who were fading from her mind had infused her with their instincts, knowledge, and wisdom that had become a part of her. But write, though she could, she could not write down an exact recipe of their nettle soup, nor their *piparkūkas*. Somehow, mysteriously, she could not pin down with a quill anything but the very basic ingredients. Therefore, when the *Henker's* wife called for her *Leben Kuchen* recipe, suddenly having lost all allergies, Mara, honestly, could not write it out. Besides, when once she did put some recipe on paper and gave it to Olga, it turned into something no one liked. From then on, the frustrated *Frau* Henker began calling Mara a liar, a deceiver, a foreigner, and finally pinned on her the label *Bakkerhexe.*

Still, the *Henker,* deaf to his complaining wife, kept sending Olga or Oleg, or both, every morning to the bakery for a basket of the *Leben Kuchen . . .* Sometimes, he went himself to see that all was as it should be and asked if she needed anything because he wanted no interruptions of the supplies. Sometimes, when he was in a good mood, he told her that he was very satisfied and pleased with her work. He even tipped his hat to her when they chanced to meet out in the open. The mayor was also satisfied. He received his daily loaf of bread, as did the priest, the judge, and the gatekeeper. So all was well. In fact, not only had Mara become the ornament of the town, but also her fame was spreading beyond the town wall. Not even a year had passed when orders started coming from many other kingdoms and the courts of Berlin.

VIII

The Bakery Expanded

Naturally, Mara could not fill the orders alone, even though some women and children helped. For her work to go smoothly, she needed guaranteed efficiency. And so, one day, she went to the mayor with a special request: she asked him if she could hire help. She would apprentice trustworthy boys and girls into the baking enterprise and form a guild. The mayor was taken aback, saying that she was a woman and to run a guild was a man's job, but his wife interrupted, saying that Mara's was a fine idea. She looked at her daughters— Johannah and Margareta—and said that they were old enough to learn a trade just in case they were left on their own and that, besides, as all know, "The way to a man's heart is through his stomach." Heinrich, too, jumped up in full support, sharpening his tools and thinking how he would always be in his lady's presence and that, in time, she would allow him to kiss more than her hand. The mayor opened and closed his mouth, but no objections passed over his lips. Suddenly, he felt he had been pushed into the forefront of a movement, a social upheaval, perhaps even a revolution. After stammering and clearing his throat, all he could say was "Where and how will it all end?" Still, he promised to take the issue up at the next town meeting.

Meanwhile, Mara asked *Frau* Mayor to make a list of girls and boys such as would be willing and able to start working. *Frau* Mayor, glad to be so entrusted, put the names of her daughters on top of a blank page and then listed others below according to her likes and dislikes. At the town meeting, the proposal was accepted without much quarrel. All were pleased that their tables would be ensured with the best baked goods and that there would be a surplus to sell, and, therefore, not only they but also the whole town would become rich and famous. While others argued and debated, the town rulers put a heavy tax on Mara and doubled the price for exports. A committee was set up to deal with the merchants who ruled the trade routes. It was suggested that a factory might be built … Oh, grand dreams and visions of fame and fortune ran in front of the grit of daily work! And in the forefront stood Mara, who had long stopped looking beyond the ominous city wall. She appeared to have become, as Heinrich had predicted, a part of Fernau, a part of the order of things and seemed quite content. She even caught herself no longer minding the wall, nor the clouds of stink. When she became aware of that, she was alarmed at the inconsistency of the human heart and mind, but she was too busy to dwell on things she could not change or understand.

Of greater concern was the mayor's wife's omission of Olga and Oleg from the list of apprentices. She knew that the twins would be too haughty to be of any real help and that all the children avoided them because they carried the smell of their slaughterhouse with them. Still … *Beware of the deadly sins of envy and jealousy,* Mara's father had said when they parted so long ago.

Not giving in to the little devils playing inside her, she designed an insignia and ordered seamstresses to make aprons and hats for everyone on the list. She had the potters make more bowls and the silversmiths make pans, spoons, and whatever a baker needed. She ordered her place enlarged and two more ovens built. All this took time, but she did not slack in her daily duties and filled all orders on time, as usual. The omission of Olga and Oleg dropped from her mind as she memorized the names of all the chosen children and learned about their homes and parents, their likes and dislikes. While waiting for the construction work, supervised by Heinrich, to be done, Mara began training her crew.

When, some months later, the remodeled bakery was opened, there was a great celebration, and Mara was honored. In her white costume, holding a bouquet of meadow flowers, she stood on the garlanded platform like a queen. Even the *Henker* gloated, while other men looked on. However, swayed by the *Henker's* wife, some women eyed the event suspiciously, jealously, but said nothing.

Once the excitement was over, work fell into a scheduled routine. Only faithful Heinrich, inside the year having changed from boy to man, was becoming more vigilant and protective of his lady and was most eager to serve her whenever she called. He guarded her with his life. He had no thoughts for anyone else, even though many maidens and their mothers cast longing glances his way. Mara was his everything. Sometimes, she teased him and laughed at his oversensitive care, but he never backed off. Like a watchdog, he sniffed the air and smelled danger. And then, one evening, as he passed the *Henker's* house, his vigilance paid off. Through the open windows, he heard angry, arguing voices, and, hiding in the shadow of a large lilac bush, he stopped to listen.

"But I can find no fault with her!" the *Henker* shouted. "I cannot simply kill people without any cause. I have my principles, a reputation to hold up, and I need her cookies!"

Heinrich held his breath and flattened himself low down by the window under the box of geraniums.

"You fool! You can always say that she is a witch." "How, you idiot?"

"Who's calling me names? You think you're so smart and powerful, you bloody man! But there's plenty you don't know. While you snore away, she concocts her dough by magic. Only witches work in the night, and no normal woman could bake like that—at least I couldn't."

"You?" sneered the *Henker*. "What you cannot do proves nothing."

The window was slammed shut, but still yelling noises leaked through the glass. Heinrich hurried away, deciding to say nothing to Mara yet but watched her more closely and from a safe distance. At the same time, he told himself not to worry about women gossiping, because he knew that they would be locked together in a yoke and would have to go about the town as long as the *Henker* ordered. Heinrich also was assured by the *Henker's* attack on his wife. He would not want to get rid of Mara because he was hopelessly addicted to the cookies she baked. Like the entire townspeople, he was spoiled by her baking and could not imagine a day without her wonder breads and cookies any more than they could imagine Fernau without its white- foamed beer. The parents of the apprentices, too, were happy to have their children employed and their futures secured. With such logic, the faithful knight convinced himself that, at least for the present, Mara was safe. Still, he remained alert. As he kept watch, there were times when he thought he heard suspicious words and saw envious glances in the eyes of the children who had not been chosen to work in what had become the best guild in town. In Mara's care, no one was hungry, cold, or beaten.

***

Inside the bakery, things went well. Mara, herself powdered with flour, leaned over her apprentices, cheerfully instructing, correcting, praising. Sometimes, she taught the children the songs she remembered and loved; sometimes, she told them stories; but mostly, she showed them, by example, the love for honest work and the joy of deserved rest at the end of a busy day. She punished no one and trusted everyone, rewarding with an extra penny those who showed initiative and imagination. She never scolded when a child made a mistake or changed a recipe more than she would like. As long as the results pleased the taste buds of the people inside and outside the great wall, no one was afraid or felt threatened.

And so another year rolled around, the hours and days passing quickly, stopping at the holy days and Sundays to rest and gather strength. By midsummer, a class of new bakers received their certificates. They proudly took them home, telling their parents that soon they would find real jobs and be rich. When that did not happen, Mara invited anyone who wished to stay on to work for her all summer. Most children chose to stay.

IX

Training of Olga and Oleg

The summer days of Mara's second year in Fernau, sweltered in heat and humidity, enclosed as they were inside the town wall. No draft from the outside aired the streets and blew away the stench that clouded around the *Henker's* house, which everyone bypassed by making extra-large loops, all in one breath, if possible. Tired and hot, people became more short-tempered, irritated, and suspicious of each other. Olga and Oleg, both having turned into stocky late teenagers, stayed inside their walled yard, watching their father butcher and execute. At the same time, they were upset that their peers did not stop to talk to them or invite them to join in games and dances.

"You have money and influence and power," growled their father. "And that is what rules the world. You, my son, will have to learn my trade—there will always be a need for an executioner. I learned the old trade from my father, and he from his. Deep roots has our family tree, and therefore you must branch out. I'll have to work harder to make a man out of you."

At first, Oleg cringed from his father's words and the future he imagined— all slimy with blood and money. But as the summer heat continued and he felt more and more isolated, his body filled with such rage and hatred that he could not wait to kill the small beasts and stray animals his father set before him. Before a month passed, he felt strange exhilaration when he saw blood run out of any creature and a greater pleasure when he felt his powerful hand invade a body and make its life stop. He realized he actually liked to see people make their loops around him and the little children scream and hide.

He enjoyed locking the gates, the houses, the halls so that no one could escape without his knowledge to breathe the evening air cooled by the winds that blew from the northern seas.

The *Henker* was pleased with his son but worried about his daughter. "She must learn a trade and also have a chance to stand on her own feet, since she will not be beautiful enough to attract either a duke or a prince, and nothing less will do," he let his wife know. "She must get into the bakery business and take over. She must learn how to bake those ginger cookies, and, if she cannot, she could simply manage and let others do the work. Our haughty Livonian herself could be her first slave. I can arrange that much, I assure you."

Olga listened through the cracks when her parents conversed in hushed tones and pictured a rosy future for herself: she saw a castle on top of a hill; she would have servants, carriages, horses; and she would dress in silks, bleached linen, fine wool, and rich furs. She would wear powdered wigs and go to courtly balls, where, soon enough, princes and princesses would notice her. The princes would come to court her, but she wouldn't settle for anybody; he would have to be handsome and powerful. Oh, how she would show all those conceited Fernau girls who was queen and who a cinder maid! Olga, like her brother, soon felt the joy of hating others. This common hatred bound the twins; it turned into a strange, exciting passion neither had experienced. They watched each other jealously and often, secretively, slept in the same bed as they had slept in the same womb. Their perverse happiness and their common hatred sustained them. They watched and listened for causes to hurt people. Strangely, but not surprisingly, their parents showed their satisfaction with approving nods. "Our children will know how to get on in this world," said the *Henker*, as he watched the townspeople and especially the children's fears and aversion whenever the twins paraded through the streets.

Softly, under closed doors and behind cupped hands, those fears and aversions spread. They accelerated after one street sweeper swore to another that she had seen crusted blood on Oleg's chin and that there were bloodstains on Olga's blouse. Soon, someone else pointed out that Olga's lips were unusually red and that her eyes shone in the dark. Naturally, the *Henker* ordered the slandering suspects to be yoked with an iron clamp that resembled a huge paperclip. Several pairs swept the streets for a fortnight yoked like that, while the *Henker* family gloated at the embarrassment and horror they had inflicted and even discussed new methods of torture and terror. But this did not stop the flow of gossip that circulated through the underground like sewage rats. The horror grew with the summer heat, and before long, people said they heard wolves howling around the city wall.

Pollution and Plague

Autumn eased the summer sultriness and, cooling the air, robed Fernau in blazing hues of gold, red, and orange. Chestnuts falling from the golden trees hit the cobblestones as leaves swooning fell over them. Boys filled their pockets with the chestnuts they would use in their slings to scare the cats and dogs and even Oleg. Still, the cries of animals being slaughtered and the stench of burning hair and nails marred the air as usual. No matter how hard Mara and company sprinkled spices, the stench could not be covered over. The *Henker,* nervous and furious, ordered the torture yoke for any pair of men and women who as much as hinted that he might have anything to do with the pollution. And if anyone suggested any evildoings by his children, he ordered the pendulum, the wheel that crushed bones, or even the basket. By All Souls' Day, several people had perished in the tower.

Mara held her mouth bridled and her eyes and ears wide open. Heinrich was never more vigilant, separating the truth from lies, now analyzing each case for her so that she would not panic and fall into the trap that *Frau* Henker slyly laid out for her. Yet her heart and soul were churning, steaming, bubbling to the dangerous point of eruption. Heinrich knew that, sooner or later, things would come to a head and his lady would have to fight for her life, and he would have to prove to her that he loved her to the end— whatever dreadful end it might be.

The crisis came when, on the eve of St. Martin's, a poor boy named Jack, an apprentice at the bakery, did not deliver the daily cookies and breads to the *Henker's* as instructed but escaped with the full basket to his parents' hut at the very edge of town. He had stolen to save his two little sisters, who were deathly ill. Their mother was too exhausted to care for them. His father lost himself in drunken stupor days on end. There was no food in the house and no fire in the hearth. Mara knew Jack to be a diligent, trustworthy worker who tried to raise himself above the family's ruin and who loved his little sisters with all his heart. She, of course, did not condone his dishonesty, but she understood and sympathized, and when she heard that Oleg had caught the boy and that there would be no mercy, she rushed to plead his case. It did no good, and poor Jack had his hands cut off. He perished with the rest of the family.

Long after the boy's soul had winged its way to some star, Mara heard his cries in the night; sometimes, she was sure she saw his thin, lanky form float through the bakery, sprinkling ashes on everything. She was afraid to bake, afraid of invisible poison, afraid that others would get ill and turn on her. She baked nothing for a fortnight, which upset everyone, most of all the *Henker*, who raged from his insatiable cravings. Desperate Heinrich was beside himself. All he could do was stay by and make his sisters take over the management of bread making so that the townspeople would be satisfied. The cookies had to wait. He had his father ring the bell and announce that Mara was ill but would soon recover, and all would be well again. But *Frau* Henker and her twins gloated, while the *Henker* pounded the table with his huge fists. Meanwhile, Mara's nerves calmed, and the night cries and floating shadows vanished.

XI

"Get The Recipe!"

"**P**lease! Go to the Bakkerhexe," Heinrich heard *Frau* Henker coax Oleg in a scratchy, malignant whisper. "Get from her the ginger cookie recipe so we don't have to run to her every time he's hungry. Olga must learn it, and then we'll see." She laughed as though she had laryngitis. Heinrich peered through the slightly ajar steaming window and saw her take a hold of Oleg's bare black-haired arm and feel his muscles. "You have become a very strong young man," she said, stroking the arm. He pulled away irritated. "Yes, you are. You are a man," she said full of meaning. "And she is a lonely woman— an old maid." She took her son's face in her hands and, smiling knowingly, petted his cheeks. "Yes, she is a woman, and a woman needs a man, we all know that." She opened his shirt and scrutinized his body the way she did when he was a baby and later, after the smallpox had left him scarred forever. "Who knows what devils she is running from, what lecheries her pretty skin covers?" She gulped beer from a bottle and laughed, tickling his armpits.

"Mother!" he yelled and pulled away.

"Well? You cannot go on playing love games only with your sister. You are not children anymore."

"Mo-other!" he tried to shout louder, but the word stuck and gurgled in his throat.

"Aha! I think you know full well what I mean." She eyed him as he clumsily looked for a way out, but she stood with her back to the closed door. "She is a lonely woman, and she must need a man. Heinrich is an ass, we all know that. He's a joke. Even she laughs at him behind his back while he slinks around her!" Hearing that, Heinrich curled his hands into tight fists, ready to strike, but all he could attack was the stinking air. "Go!" *Frau* Henker spoke like to a dog. "Go to her and ask her for the recipe, and if she don't give it to you, then take her, damn it! Surprise her. You know, the way a real man hunts. Get her when she's off guard. Women really like that. They like forceful men."

Oleg pushed her aside and stumbled out the door. Heinrich followed, sliding along the shadows, not knowing what to do, until both men stood a short distance from each other near the bakery. Heinrich, behind the chestnut tree, saw Oleg straighten up as a soldier poised for attack and cross the street. He stretched one leg forward, ready to intercept but then stopped and fell back behind the large trunk of the tree and spied wide-eyed as Oleg pushed his way inside the bakery. He heard and saw nothing. The shutters were closed; only the two hearts shone bright yellow. He knew that the apprentices would be gone, and Oleg might pretend that he had come to lock the door. He waited in suspense for Oleg to come out, but, instead, the light was blown out of one of the hearts.

***

As Oleg had crossed the street with large, impatient strides, pumped up by his mother's commands, he imagined Mara resting, taking off her flour- dusted cap, washing her face, unbraiding and brushing her thick brown hair that would shroud the best part of her body. *Get her when she least expects it,* his mother's voice rang in his ears. *Now!*

Like a bloodthirsty bat, he then moved toward the lone flickering amber heart. All the anger, lust, visions, and revenge he had nurtured for many nights and days pushed him forward. When he knocked on the door, Mara opened it. Startled, she tried to close it, but he was already inside. "I have come to ask a favor," he said quite kindly. "On behalf of my mother, actually," he said louder and moved a step farther. Disappointed, he saw that she was still fully dressed; her hair, tightly braided, crowned her head. Her apron was tightly tied, and she held a heart-shaped cookie cutter in one hand. A sheet of rolled-out dough with heart cutouts covered her worktable.

"No. I cannot and will not give it to you no matter for whom it may be."

He explained more clearly his purpose, saying that his mother only wanted Olga to learn how to make the ginger cookies, but Mara shook her head, saying that it was too complicated and that Olga would not be able to follow it. Oleg pushed forward, making her step backward, where the oven still glowed. "Your sister doesn't have my hands, nor my heart," Mara said frightened. "Even if she tried very, very hard, she could not make them come out right. Your father wouldn't like them and would only be disappointed and angry. So, please, leave me alone! I'll keep baking them as always. I promise to have a fresh batch every morning, if it's that important, but I'm afraid that he'll suffer from too much sweetness," she talked rapidly, in streams, pushing him back with her words and reason, keeping the sound of her voice between them. But before she could utter another word, Oleg flattened her against a wall. He was pressing his bulk against her, one arm crushing her shoulders, while the other slid down her back, the hand lifting her skirt, his mouth hunting her lips, silencing them with fierce thrusts. Struggling, her knee kicked his aggressive hardness as her hand, her fingers wrapped around the cookie cutter, pushed forward until she felt his hot blood in her palm.

"You damned witch!" Oleg yelled, releasing her and pulling the cookie cutter out of his cheek and dashing it against the wall. "You'll pay for this! Now you've branded me for life, you foreign devil, and I won't rest until I've hunted you down like the sly fox you are!"

Mara soaked a rag and threw it at him, ordering him to get out.

"You'll regret this, you *Bakkerhexe*! I'll get you yet, I swear!" He cursed and spewed more bloody invectives as he stumbled out the door, where the darkness hid him.

Minutes later, Heinrich rushed up to the bakery and knocked softly on the door. But Mara did not open it. He sat down on the threshold and waited, tapping at intervals, but still, she did not show herself. After the moon had reached its zenith, he gave up and slowly walked home. At a turn, he saw Oleg stumbling out of the pub and turned back to take up his watchman's post by the bakery, waiting. But Oleg never showed up. Heinrich dozed at Mara's doorstep until the break of dawn and then walked home.

***

Late the next afternoon, Heinrich passed the *Henker's* house and again heard the *Frau* shouting, "Go back to the witch! Get the recipe, you fool!" He stood still in the early darkness, listening for more, but Oleg's hand slammed the shutters.

As if attacked, Heinrich started running. He ran straight for the bakery. The door opened as the apprentices came out. He waited for them to pass and then walked up the steps and slid inside, startling Mara. In the musty darkness, Heinrich pained, "It's started."

"What?"

"The witch hunt." In out-of-breath phrases, he told her what he had heard.

"I am aware of it. Oleg was here last night and asked me for my *Leben Kuchen* recipe, and I refused, and then he called me a witch, and that was that." Mara said. "But I will not give in. I will not be bullied and assaulted. There still is a God, and he must rule the world. There still are good people in this town," she said firmly.

Then Heinrich took a strong hold of her hand. "Oh," he sighed. "They will not give up. They who want to hurt you will have their way. They are laying the snares, greasing the ropes." He guided her hands to his cheeks, his lips. Her hands froze, while his burned. "The *Henker* will not be humiliated," he spoke into her open palms. "Not again. He will not give up. He knows the townspeople are on your side. He knows they love you and hate and fear him. He sees how we all hate Olga and Oleg."

"I don't hate them, not really," Mara said softly, feeling her blood rise to her face. "Oleg is just a clumsy, uncivil, spoiled boy."

"But let me put a bolt on your door so he cannot barge in like he did last night."

"You saw him?" "Yes."

"So why didn't you come to my rescue, brave knight?"

He stood up and reached for his tools. "I was too late. Your house was dark, and when I knocked, you didn't open the door. Why?"

"Have you also come to trouble me? All I wanted was peace, and that is all I will tell you now. But it would be nice if you could put a strong bolt on my door."

Feeling set free, he started working, while Mara continued to clean up. "He was here a long time."

"As long as he needed … Do you always spy on me?"

"No. But I often walk by just to make sure that all is well. I saw him walk into your house and wanted to stop him, but … I …"

"Couldn't, right?" Mara looked at him as he tested the bolt. "Afraid, yes? Well, all he wanted was my recipe, and we talked, but he didn't get anything, and I think I taught him a lesson and he will leave me alone."

"It's not only him," Heinrich stumbled on. "It's the whole family. The whole system. It's the way they work so they can have their way. That's what you are up against … That's what this whole town is up against."

"Well, then I must teach the young man and his family some rules of civility and respect for the rights of others, and you must protect and defend me—even to your parents, because it seems that they are not as cordial as they used to be."

"Ha!" he laughed. "It's hopeless. They are scared or just careful, I don't know!" Heinrich reached again for her hands, but she put them behind her back. "Forgive me," he pleaded, "but you—we—must not give up hope. You're so right about many things, only they don't understand. The time will come when I will get you out of this town and hide you, even if they kill me. I'll take you across the borders into some other kingdom where no *Henkers* rule. I swear!"

Mara petted his cheek lightly and said that she would always leave the cellar trapdoor unbolted and will always bolt the main door. Then she asked him to leave and opened the door. The night was very dark, full of rain clouds the wind tossed about.

"Beware of Oleg," Heinrich warned as he stepped over her threshold and looked both ways before he crossed the street.

"Oh, I'm not afraid," she lied and quickly went inside and bolted her door.

XII

The Enlightened

But she was afraid and troubled. After she had finished cleaning up and eaten her soup, she sat down with her sketchbook and paints, trying to decide how to decorate the display window for the fast-approaching Advent season. But no ideas came; nothing could blot out Oleg's intrusion and Heinrich's warning. Oleg's bloody shout *"Bakkerhexe!"* rang in her ears, accusing and calling her as from a dark pit. Shivering, she stood up and stretched. She paced restlessly, expecting the door to break open at any moment and her tyrant or victim to barge in like a gust of cold wind. Mindlessly, she unbolted the door and waited. As nothing happened, she quickly wrapped herself in her hooded cape, took a small bag of assorted cookies, and went to the library. After greeting the librarian kindly and giving him his bribe, she asked the timid, staring man if he had any documents about recent witch trials. Did he have any information about the trial of a Katharina Schraderin, commonly known as *Bakkerhexe?*

The nearsighted man eyed her questioningly and then nodded and disappeared among the shelves. At last, he came out with a folder and handed it over, saying that she must keep their transaction a secret. Leaning over the desk, he whispered, "I trust you, for you, too, belong to us, the *Illuminati.*" When she returned a puzzled look, he added, whispering that in any darkness, there is always light and that among people of dark minds, there are enlightened ones, and, "I can tell by the light in your eyes that you are among the *Illuminati.* I have been curious about you ever since you arrived, ever since you have been borrowing our books. But do be careful! The darkness inside these walls is very great, and the witch hunts are not really over. Never will be, only they will take new forms and find new victims, such as mysterious strangers or healers or …" he paused, "bakers." He leaned toward her. "I know about the *Henker*. Know all about him and his family. He's been here from childhood. We are about the same age. Went to school together, but he did not have a good head for learning. Comes from a long line of head choppers, but wasn't a bad-looking young man, so the girls liked him, and he ended up marrying one of our classmates, the pampered daughter of our banker. She is used to having her way, so do be careful."

Nervously, Mara told him that she was not interested in people's gossip and that she believed the witch hunts were over and are being outlawed.

"But they still happen, especially in closed-off places, like our town."

"Where there are no such things as witches, ghosts, goblins, or werewolves."

"One can never be sure," the librarian said and added, "What is and what people want to believe are not always the same … I see and hear things."

Mercifully, the door opened, and a schoolteacher entered, lifting his hat to Mara as she, securing the folder inside her cape, thanked the librarian and hurried out the door.

She walked cautiously back to her house and bolted the door. In the candlelit darkness, where the oven embers still glowed, she took off her cape, covered her shoulders with a shawl, and, settling at her desk, lit a candle. Like some sacred scroll, she unwound the folder and browsed through it. She read general essays dealing with foregone witch trials, the Inquisition, and the Church. She looked for Livonia and found out that "*the official statement regarding witches and witchcraft was issued in 1480 throughout The Holy Roman Empire.*" Therefore, she reasoned, it pertained also to Livonia. The main points were

1. Witches have signed agreements with the devil and are leading immoral l

2. Witches reject Christian religion and the teachings of the Church cooperate with evil powers.

3. With the help of secret powers, witches harm people and destroy property

4. Witches fly through the air and may turn themselves and others into creatures.

She read on:

"Witches and wizards were those who have contacts with the devil and evil spirits. Therefore, those people who are regarded as such are dangerous, and decent people should not have any contact with them. They are incarnated by evil … With that, as is known, began witch-hunts with their burnings, judgments, etc. …"

She paused. "So this is history. This was true also in Livonia, but—thanks be to God—not as much as in Germany, Spain, and other places, yet even one unjust torture is too much," she argued in the darkness as if she were on trial. "*There were quite a few witch-hunts and legal proceedings in Riga from around 1646 to 1650.*" She copied that statement in red ink.

"And I was born in 1647! Right at the start there, in Livonia, but what happened here? Even before I turned sixteen, the hideous word *Bakkerhexe* was first hurled at me, and then it became louder and louder and more and more nasty. *She* said it—my stepmother, the real witch. And my father could do nothing about it. So here I am."

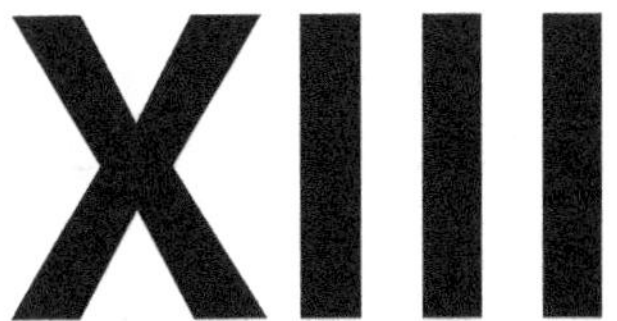

Reflections

She fixed her eyes on the silent, unruly flame of the candle, slowly caking with wax, and remembered:

It—the scream—happened on the morning of Mara's sixteenth birthday. They were eating the birthday *kriŋgelis (an* oversized sweet dough pretzel). When finished, *Herr* Liebman gave her a large box, beautifully wrapped. In it lay a blue dress of simple cut, trimmed in white. "Oh, *mein Herr,* how beautiful!" Mara exclaimed. "As beautiful as this spring morning."

"And you're even lovelier than this whole day," the baron said after she kissed his hand. *Frau* Liebman, Angelina, and Sophia looked on, their faces flushed and eyes glowing. Fortunately, any forthcoming, embarrassing scene was blocked when a servant came in to clear the table. Quickly, as if trying to escape an oncoming storm, the baron excused himself and, wishing his women a happy day, departed. When the clicking of his boots had receded, Mara, aware of three pairs of eyes full of hatred, gathered her birthday present ready to leave, but Stepmother lifted herself up and shouted, *"Du Hexe!"* with such venom that her lips overflowed with saliva. Waving her fan like a flyswatter, she threatened to slap Mara down. Angelina and Sophia grinned as at a circus show, while Mara didn't know where to go and what to say. For a moment, she stood still, taking in the mad scene. When it would not blow over, she turned and left the room. As usual when troubled, she escaped to the forest down beyond the castle garden and the playground.

Once under the protective branches full of singing, chirping birds, she turned off on an overgrown path that snaked along the riverbank, past deep sandstone caves, where long ago, it was believed, witches hid out. The story had traveled by word of mouth, telling that once upon a time, when a plague broke out in the region, the people blamed the *raganas* and hunted them down. They raided the caves, burned down the woods, and the *raganas*—so people believed still to this day—had turned into wild ducks and flown away, all except the leader, who was burned in the town's square. Although the hunts had happened so long ago and that fact became legend, still superstitions lived on, and normal folk stayed away from the deep woods on the other side of the river, where they knew the wild beasts roamed and thieves hid out.

Not believing everything she heard, Mara, two springs ago, after her fourteenth birthday and after another unwarranted scolding, had run away from the castle, crying that she'll never come back. She ran out of the Liebman estate and soon found herself up against the river, turbulent and high. Carefully, she walked along the river and then up the bank and down again to where the river narrowed. Across it lay a fallen tree. On the other side, she saw an overgrown cave and close to it a column of smoke curling up to the sky. *They didn't all fly away,* she observed and, driven by greater curiosity than caution, spread her arms for balance and walked across the log, cautiously pushing forward.

Through a thicket of leafing bracken, she saw strange women sitting in a circle in front of the cave. They had open books on their laps, and they were taking turns reading. She crept up closer and hid behind a large tree. *Raganas.* She held her breath, holding on to a branch. The branch cracked, and she fell forward, grabbing on to the twigs of a bush from which darted out some crows, causing an old *ragana* to jump up. Stepping forward, she saw the girl entangled in the thicket like a lost deer, while the other women ran inside the cave.

"Ah, what do we have here?" the Old One cooed. "A pretty little *Spīgaliņa* (firefly)! Come! Come on closer, you blithe spirit! You're one of us, I can tell. The wind carried you here. You're brave and clever, yes, yes, I know, I see. I can feel the flames of your restless soul that has no home, no mother, poor child." Mara stepped back, but the Old One stepped up closer, beckoning. As if her long finger were a hook or magnet, Mara couldn't resist. "Yes, yes, don't be afraid. Come and rest, dear child," she coaxed. "You must be tired and thirsty. Here, drink from my cup the sweet juice from the breast of Mother Earth. It's good. It will refresh you and give you strength drawn right from the heart of the earth. You're pale. You need it."

Mara drank, and sure enough, with each sip, she felt pleasant currents flowing through her body, washing all fears away. She asked what the strange drink was made of, and the Old One told her that it was last summer's berry juice, fermented and strong, but when Mara asked for more, she shook her finger, saying, "No, no! Only a small draught for one so young. We welcome you."

The Old One clapped her hands, and the other women came out of the cave, cautiously in a row, one by one. Mara eyed them suspiciously. They were a motley crew. Some were dark skinned, others pale; some with long black hair, others with wild red curls, and still others with flaxen braids down to the waist, and then there was one with her hair shaved off, bald like the moon. They mumbled and spoke in a mix of words Mara didn't understand, and when she stepped back, trying to figure out how to run away, they laughed in a gurgling, coughing chorus. One with the dark skin and wild hair pulled her by the hand. Another said in a coarse voice, "Sisters, don't you see? She's afraid. She thinks that we are some *raganas,* don't you, pretty girl?"

"If you're not, then who are you? Why do you live here?" Mara asked.

Not then but the next time Mara showed up, the Old One explained. "My girls are a sad lot," she began, lit her pipe, and sat down on a stump, pulling Mara next to her.

"They all have escaped something or other," the Old One began. "Some ran away from husbands, some from captivity. You know, when our soldiers go to war, they kill as many men as they can and grab whatever they can find and then take the women and children captive. Last, they burn down the houses and even whole villages. The miserable women become slaves and are beaten, molested, and tormented in many ways that you are too young to understand. Some are accused of witchcraft and tortured. They are tested by water and fire, and when they fail the tests, they are burned. Then the priests praise their God for delivering them from devils … Oh, no, we are nothing supernatural, only troubled and tormented women with no home and no families to shelter us. Some are smart, very clever and cunning, but they can also rage and howl like mad wolves. They can hurt and attack when provoked, so you must be careful and always be kind."

"Yes. But you?" Mara asked. "Who are you?"

"My dear child, I see that you are bound for trouble," she said, puffing on the pipe, eyeing and evaluating. "But you ask," she puffed, "and I must answer ... So ... many years ago, when I wasn't much older than you, there was a hunt for *raganas*. It was up north in Libland. Somehow, the Crusaders had missed our region, and so we were still faithful to our gods and goddesses. But some soldiers came upon us and told the bishop, who popped up the next day with a couple of priests. The bishop ordered his soldiers to turn all the village folk into Christians. The men then started to dunk us into the river. We kicked and screamed. Our men with shovels, axes, and forks came and fought the army, but, naturally, they were overpowered and killed one by one. They burned down our houses and, as I told you the other day, tied up the women, my mother among them, and us the children. Well, that's all. They treated us badly. Some years later, my mother died. I was grown up—like you—not anymore a child and not yet a woman, but I knew what men did to women ... I heard my mother cry so that those cries still ring in my ears ... So—one night, urged by others, I escaped, and we roamed around until they were after us again. And again, I escaped. Well, it's a long story. You needn't know everything, only that now I help other women. I learned from an older woman how to be a healer, and now I can teach others and give advice. I help those who want to be helped. I teach them to read and write, and when they are ready, there are people—good, sincere Christian sisters and brothers—who help us. You understand, it's all done in secret because of superstitious people who spy on us and cry, "*Ragana!*" every time a cow gets sick or the wind blows the wrong way. But there are people with light in their minds and hearts who want to help the misfortunate find a way out. They find safe places in convents or wherever. I don't know what happens to them, but there are many who find me and thank me. So here I am. I can help you too. But if you turn me in, I will hunt you down, that I promise." She said this leaning forward, glaring, shaking her finger. Hot and icy currents stormed through Mara's body so that she was afraid she would faint. The Old One braced her with one arm and made her take a drink from the breast of Mother Earth. Revived, Mara sat up.

"Swear that you will not betray us," hissed the Old One, and Mara swore, crossing her heart, in the name of Holy Mary. Then the *ragana* smiled and let her have another drink.

"Read! You must learn to read, dear child!" she said after a while, "and I will teach you—Latin and German, the rest you can figure out for yourself. Letters are letters, and I see that you have a good head."

From then on, Mara visited the cave as often as the weather permitted and when she could safely leave the castle. Stepmother and stepsisters knew that she always took long afternoon walks while *Mutti* napped and they stitched their tapestries, so no one paid any attention to Mara's coming and going. *Herr* Liebman was usually out on business.

Mara learned quickly, not only reading and counting but also many other things. The Old One taught her some secrets about herbs and cures. A younger one taught her hands how to form letters and write sentences with a quill on paper or birch bark. They let her borrow books with poems and stories, which thrilled Mara and fired her imagination so that she became restless and wished to see the world beyond her mountains and woods. Often, when lonely, she would go up in the tower room to read and, studying the pictures in the books, tried drawing what she imagined; she also learned to stitch simple scenes on scraps of discarded cloth the manor seamstress left behind. Excited and pleased, she showed the Old One her drawings and embroidery and received praises: "To you, dear girl, our fortune goddess Laima has given many gifts, and who knows how the Lord of heaven and earth will use your hands."

At that, Mara smiled, eager to learn and do more, and so, as time went on, she and the *raganas* had many interesting conversations about strange places and people who studied the rules and secrets of nature and made books in every language of the world. She also learned about the rules of the church and how many women were burned as witches. When Mara wanted to know if there really were such creatures as witches, the *raganas* laughed at the whole idea, saying that all the women who were so called and were pushed out of society and forced to live in the woods were strong and smart, smarter than other women and the men who chased them down. Ignorant people were afraid and therefore said stupid things, the Old One explained. Still, stupidity and ignorance are powerful weapons that can kill, she said and warned Mara again and again to watch out and be careful and not tell anyone where she learned the things she knew.

"But," said the Old One, "We must do everything possible to spread knowledge so that the light of the spirit would dispel all darkness. Only ignorant people can be manipulated into believing such things as are told about us."

Mara didn't go about spreading knowledge but tried to avoid Stepmother and sisters as much as she could without being noticed. But eventually, they noticed. They watched her and saw that she had changed. The sun and wind had tanned her face, and her eyes shone with a knowing light. Their insults did not seem to affect her. She didn't cringe in fear but stood straight in a provocative, challenging attitude, which provoked Stepmother out of control. With her evil eyes, she saw that next to Mara, her daughters had no chance of catching a prince or even a duke, and it was then she started calling her *Hexe*, at first in muffled tones but soon loudly and even in the presence of the baron. He could not stop her.

For the rest of the summer, Mara stopped going to the cave as often and took shorter, irregular walks around the Liebman estate. When the cold winds and rains brought in autumn, the river rose dangerously. Mara knew that the log would be slippery and impossible to cross and, taking no chances, stayed close to home. However, on one golden late September day, after an early frost had glazed the ground, she put on her warm cape and went out. As before, she took the path leading to the cave, but when she came to the river crossing and saw the log glazed with ice, she stopped and looked. She called, "*Oo-oo,*" and listened. Only a soft echo answered. The cave gaped open and mute. There was no sign of life, no movement, no fire or smoke. She knew they were gone, flown away—perhaps like cranes—to warmer lands, such as she read about in books.

***

But birds come back ... and again, curiosity driven, Mara took the path she had left two years ago until she saw the line of red sandstone caves. The crossing log lay half under water. As then, there was still no sign of human life on the other side. Tired, thinking, and reminiscing, she leaned against a tree when a woodsman startled her. Clearly, he came from the Livonian village, but Mara was afraid and, turning, ran back up the path, her hair and skirt blowing in the wind, leaving the man far behind. She slowed down when she came upon a sunny spot, blue with anemones. She stooped down and picked a handful and, for a moment, lay down on the warm ground and turned her face to the sun. Rested, she walked on, listening to the music of the forest, when through the barren trees, she saw bent-over peasant women picking anemones. Suddenly, they straightened up, as if rising from the earth, and watched Mara leap over a low spot and run down a ravine.

She came up on the back side of the castle and went in through the service door. Quietly, she tiptoed down the hall toward *Herr* Liebman's study and cautiously pushed the door open, wanting to put the anemones—as was her duty—at the foot of the alabaster bust of a woman.

When Mara was about ten years old, *Herr* Liebman had put the statue in that corner and assigned her to dust it and see to it that there were fresh flowers or evergreen branches in the small and larger vases. Little Mara was happy to please the master and always obeyed him because he had brought her to the castle after her mother died and was always kind to her. But when she asked him who the lady was, he only stroked the alabaster shoulders and said that she was only a work of art, such as she had seen in the showcases in Riga. Afraid to bother the baron, Mara asked no more questions but silently wiped off any speck of dust that dared to settle on the white face and shoulders. When she was lonesome and mistreated, she would run to the statue and tell her about the pain in her heart. She imagined the *White Lady,* as she had named her, speaking and comforting her gently from her high pedestal. Once she had fallen asleep at the pedestal, where Stepmother found her and whipped her on the behind, but that did not stop her from visiting and praying to the statue as if she were the Virgin Mary.

Now, coming in from the cold, Mara stopped short when she saw the baron standing at the bust, his hand resting on the white head. Startled, he turned, his hand quickly brushing his eyes. Embarrassed, Mara excused herself, saying that she wanted to say a poem or sing to her the song her mother always sang on her birthday. The baron smiled and stepped aside as she laid the anemones on the pedestal's narrow ledge and then, excusing herself, rose to leave, but he took her hand and drew her close to him, saying, "This is your mother … and I am your father."

"I have always wished it would be so, my lord."

"I am not surprised. You are now grown up and much too quickly."

Needing nothing more to say, they stood facing the white bust, as they also had often stood at her grave. In that pose, Angelina caught them and quickly dashed away.

***

That same spring, after the equinox, the snows melted faster than usual, and with that, the forest awakened earlier from its winter sleep. Mara, conscious of being sixteen and the daughter of her lord and master, walked with surer steps and spoke in surer accents. She went openly into the forest to pick early pussy willow and birch branches to set them at the pedestal of her mother's bust and watched the buds open up and send out their tiny leaves and yellow catkins like greetings from heaven, where she believed her mother lived and watched over her from windows draped with clouds. Nothing gave her greater joy than those walks in woodlands, where heaven was just above the trees and starlings sang their little hearts out and where everything stirred with the excitement of new life. At times, she walked to the caves but found them empty, still gaping like bewitched mouths and eyes. Then feeling a strange chill go through her, she hurried back to safer ground.

At this pregnant time of year, she would also see peasants in the birch growth, drawing sap in wooden buckets and loading them on to horse-drawn wagons to be taken away to distilleries. The sap was turned into a much- desired healthy drink all enjoyed, especially *Herr Von* Liebman. Whenever the workers saw Mara, they tipped their hats and bowed, but she hurried on, not wanting to be stopped or spoken to. Also, in the sunny spots, there would be older women with children picking flowers they would take to sell in the market. They, too, nodded and curtsied as she passed by, admiring Mara, who, like a haughty Flora or some enchanted princess, had stepped out of the pages of picture books. Mara did not know any of the women by name, but they all knew her and liked to remind each other about her scandalous mother and the baron. With keen interest, they watched this wonder—the sinful love child of the barons' rights—*Herr Von* Liebman had claimed on the peasant bride's wedding night. Some watched her with great curiosity, while others with envy. Some pitied the poor betrayed husband with whom their men had plowed the fields, while others understood full well why the bride would rather sleep in a feather bed than on a sack of straw. But Mara was not able to see the accusing glances or hear suspicious comments as she walked in the twilight between two worlds, as between night and day.

As people's moods changed, so did the weather. At the end of that same April, frost struck the land. Snow fell, and tender shoots froze. On one of those befogged mornings, at breakfast, one of the maids blurted out, saying that *raganas* have been seen in the woods. Some woodsmen, she said, had seen one trying to leap across the river close to the caves, and some women had seen them walking around along the ravines and in the birch groves. Hearing that, Mara sat up as if soused by cold water. Her cheeks burned, and her heart fluttered like a caged bird. Stepmother saw it all and, gloating, helped herself to a newly laid boiled egg. With narrowing eyes, she watched Mara blush and ate slowly, enjoying the scene. When it was over, she motioned to her daughters to leave the table. They rose and, casting accusing backward glances, went out the door.

After this, Mara didn't go into the woods but stayed on the estate grounds, watching the gardeners mulch around the roses. Soon, as is usual with the weather, the cold spell passed, and the farmhands returned to the fields. But, again, in early May came another freeze and killed the seedlings. And then again, the people started talking and wondering why they were cursed. The old folk remembered famines and plagues and were afraid. "Why, oh, why?" the lords and the servants lamented and, in the end, cursed and blamed the *raganas.*

When that cold front passed and the sun shone down on the pained earth, Mara could not hold out any longer and went to find out what was happening at the caves, and, sure enough, there they were. Seeing her across the river, the Old One waved her arms like crossing signals. She ran to the water's edge and stood at the partly submerged log and reached out, coaxing and calling, saying they crossed the waters safely and so could she. The Old One assured Mara that she, too, had the power to balance herself without slipping. But, terrified, Mara shouted, "Be careful! It's starting!" and, turning about, disappeared among the trees. On the way back, she saw again the same peasant women picking flowers. Surprised, they stood up and boldly watched her run and leap out of sight.

That evening, Stepmother stormed again and again, pointing her finger, called out, *"Hexe!* See what you've done!" She yelled at the baron and then at Mara, "Don't come near us! Don't sit at our table!" She forbade her to wander about in the woods and along the river's bank "and carry the curse on you into our castle! … To punish you for all the shame you've brought to this house and family, I order you to work in the kitchen and stay with your own kind!"

Mara looked at her father for help, but he hung his head and then, rising, said, "I agree with *Frau* Liebman that you must not wander about and out of our palace grounds. It is much too dangerous. I trust that you will respect and obey our rules. And now, if you all will excuse me, I must attend to my duties."

***

Mara, after she recovered from the attack and the baron's so openly siding with his wife and treating her like a child, submitted to her fate. Truth be told, she didn't mind working in the kitchen along with the Livonian servants, where she felt protected and warm. Besides, she learned much from the women as they cooked and baked and talked in their language—her mother's language—she hardly remembered and had not used since she stopped going to the caves. In the steam, spice, and smoke-filled kitchen, the language felt right. The women's talking sounded like choir chants she had heard in the cathedral in Riga, and, fascinated, she would often stop her work and listen, listen for the melody of the words and phrases and try to pick it all up to save and treasure. In such atmosphere and spirit, she learned quickly not only about the origins of the common people and ancient tribal wars but also about food preparation. And it was not long before she became aware that she, unlike the other cooks, had a special knack for combining unusual fruits, vegetables, spices, and various other common ingredients and turning them into rare and tasty dishes that delighted important guests and especially her father.

She showed off that special talent on her father's birthday, which was at the end of May. To please him and hoping to gain favor with her stepmother and stepsisters as well, she surprised him, the family, and his guests with a marvelous many-layered torte and a "Happy Birthday" song in the *Lettish*. He praised her, saying that only angels could have taught her to sing and bake like that and called her blessed, but *Frau* Liebman, losing her temper, pushed her piece aside and forbid her daughters to eat *"the devil's food,"* saying it would make them sick. *Herr* Liebman was outraged and ashamed, the guests were embarrassed, but Mara, her head raised and shoulders straight, walked out of the room. Thereafter, she stopped showing off and tried to blend in, but, as if other hands worked through her, everything she prepared carried its unusual flavors that made no one sick or fat. In time, even Stepmother could find no reason not to partake. Instead, she put more demands on her and kept her under control with abusive words no one should hear or read.

The Livonian kitchen women, distrusting and hating their ruling aristocrats and their usurped privileges, openly admired Mara's work and teasingly started calling her *mūsu raganiņa* (our dear little witch, an endearing form of *ragana*, but still translates into *Hexe*). When Mara, as if singed, wiped her tears, the cook, who was the first to say the word, explained that *raganas* and *ragani* to the *real* people of Livonia were honored as *clever, all-seeing blessed women and men*. They were the teachers and healers—the cook went on—the wise men and women to whom people turned for help and advice, believing that the goddesses Mara and Laima had chosen them and blessed their hands; all the people—except the foreign invaders—honored them. "Therefore, we mean no harm, but we honor you and know that our goddesses have swaddled you with their blessed powers when they visited you at the cradle." Hearing that, Mara remembered the Old One and asked the cooks to tell more stories and old tales.

That was enough prompting for the oldest cook to join in and explain how the whole concept about *raganas* changed when the old tribes were conquered and the altars of their old gods destroyed. The wars had been bloody and fierce, lasting for decades as one tribe after another was overcome and baptized in icy waters. The bishops made the conquered denounce their gods and take up the cross of their foreign three-part God named Jesus Christ, or else they would burn in hell. "So our people had to submit, take up the heavy cross, and work for their masters … But what did the crusaders know about us? What do our lords and barons understand now?" the cook asked. "Yes, we obey, for what else can we do? Actually, many of our forbearers pitied and loved this Jesus, who was nailed to the cross and who suffered for the things he didn't do, like many of us—even you—have to suffer for what you are not guilty. So we have nothing against *him*, and I believe that he doesn't mind that we love our Laima and Mara like we love and adore his blessed Mother Mary. So it's not against the Lord of Heaven we rise up but his crusaders who stole our land and killed our men and made our women widows and our children orphans. Yes, those men made our people their slaves," she said, her face burning. "It is the so-called servants of God who tried to eliminate all of us they called *pagāni*. Pagans. Yes, that is what they called our brave heroes we sing about. And they killed and cheated our cleverest merchants and warriors, because had they lived and been able to defend our land, we would surely have become a strong nation. And so the mighty, power-hungry Church that calls itself holy and an Arm of the Lord many years ago proclaimed that all wisdom comes only from the one Christian God and the Holy Bible. They singled out and accused the *raganas* and *ragani* as working together with the devil and blamed on them any troubles on land and sea and air. When the official decree against *raganas* was passed, life for our wise people became dangerous, and many fled the country, while others hid in woods and caves. It was the pagans' power and wisdom the enemy feared. And—you certainly know it—wise people are hard to rule, so they persecute and kill them to scare everybody who stands in the way. But one day, after our people will have learned from the oppressors the ways of the new world, they will wake up and fight for what is right. And they will win. Oh, yes! Our people will live again!" She beat the dough with her fists and then gently smoothed it out with buttered hands. "I won't see the day, but it will come." She wiped her hands and the sweat off her face. "But—I better not talk so much and mind my soup," she said lightheartedly and started chopping at the side of a wild boar.

When Mara wanted to know more, the kitchen women told her horror stories about how *raganas* were burned in the Riga square and other places and how they had seen those fires with their own eyes. "*Ak vai!* But that happened ages ago," one cried out.

"Yet it is not over and could happen again, even on our castle grounds," said another. And then the kitchen women talked more, some whispering, others making jokes, disbelieving that there were people who still believed that *raganas* flew around at night and brought harm to people and animals, and that was why, to scare them off, people tied bunches of red clover on their gate posts at Midsummer Night's Eve. The cooks assured Mara that they didn't believe any of the nonsense that was passed around by superstitious people but that they liked the customs and songs of that magic night "just like our noble lord, who used to go down to the valley to watch us work and listened to our singing … Yes, I remember how handsome he was but seemed very sad."

At that, the others eyed Mara knowingly and kneaded and pounded their dough harder. Smiling, Mara said that she also liked the solstice celebrations, when all the peasants danced and sang until sunrise. She did not confess that on the magic night, when people said the fern bloomed and young lovers wandered about searching for the magic blossom, strange excitement, like some mysterious hook, seemed to pull her back to the woods and caves. She did not tell them that once, when she was about thirteen, one of the Livonian maids had helped her make a flower wreath and asked her to go with her down in the valley and join the singing, but when *Herr* Liebman saw her all dressed up with a daisy garland on her head, her face blushing in excitement, he forbid her to leave the castle. She would tell nobody that later on, after crying in her room and being scolded by her stepmother, she had crept up the dark stairs to the room in the turret so she would be able to look down and listen to the singing below. Taken aback, she had bumped into *Herr* Liebman, who was standing in the open window. Not saying a word, he put his arm out and drew her to himself. Together, they looked down and listened to the singing. She asked him why he was sad. He did not answer.

But now she was sixteen. From the very start as lord of the castle, *Herr* Liebman allowed his servants to end their work at noon on the eve of the summer solstice and prepare for the celebration. Mara, her baking and cheese-binding finished, also sat singing with other cooks and servants at the edge of a meadow and made herself a garland of mixed flowers and an oak garland for the baron. In the evening, after the sauna, she put on a dress the old cook had helped her make in her spare time. It was white linen with colored designs along the borders—*Your Way*, the cook called it, as together they stitched the stars and the crosses, the moons and the suns, the trees and flowers. "These are the ancient designs that only the wise *ragani* and scribes could read. They all are long gone, and there is no one who can read what we stitch and weave. Still, you must learn them and keep the way," the kind woman said, as they hurried to finish the dress by midsummer night. "You are Mara, and in your name is magic," she heard again, looking at her hands.

When the castle was quiet and *Frau* Liebman with her daughters gone away to her parents' manor, as was their habit, Mara, all dressed up, went up to the tower, knowing that *Herr* Liebman would be there, as he was every year. She put the oak-leaf crown on his head and set down a special wheel of cheese and a pitcher of beer. Happy and surprised, he opened his arms to her and pulled her to his heart. His embrace was so tight and so warm that a never- before felt tremor went through her. As if the same wave like lightning went also through him, his arms slackened, releasing her. Awkwardly, he kissed her cheek, and his hands went up and pulled the pagan crown off his head and hung it on a peg. "Until the next year," he said in a jovially affected tone and opened the window wider. The cool breeze came up with the songs in an endless medley, one after the other, seducing and abetting the mystic mood that begged for intimacy. To break out of it, they put their hands to the bread and cheese and mugs of beer. Relaxed, leaning back, they talked about little things, looking out at the star-sown sky made bright by a lonely moon. When Mara refilled his mug, he looked up in her averted eyes, took a deep breath, and said, "Now that you are grown up and will understand—if not completely, then later in your life, which I may not live to see."

"Oh, my lord, but you're not ill?" Mara whispered and put her hand over his.

"No, dearest, but one never knows. And there will never be a better time than this enchanting night to bring her back. So listen to the story I shall tell you … about me and … your mother." He stood up and went to the window. Looking down, he told her that on such a night, seventeen years ago, he had gone down and brought up to the tower the most beautiful and chaste maiden of his domain.

"I was thirty, young and handsome, if I may say so myself. I'd been married for over ten years and was not happy with my wife, Ursula, whom I hadn't chosen—as you know only too well. In truth, we didn't know each other except from a distance. But, of course, our German superclass that ruled the land sticks together. Ursula's parents governed over Sigulda, mine over this

manor here in Wenden. Our borders were common, and our parents were friends, and so, when the time came, they decided that I and Ursula should be wed, so that our borders would be strong and our power against the often- unruly natives solid. And so we were married. The wedding ceremony was splendid. Oh, Ursula Schlim was nice enough at first and not bad looking, but it wasn't long before I discovered that her name matched her character only too accurately. She had a vile temper that often went out of control and like a raging storm came over me without warning. When that happened, she frightened and belittled me without mercy—as you see it even now when she turns on you like lightning hitting a barn, and then you run. Well, I also ran… Naturally, I could not bring myself to love her as I understood married people should. Then she laughed, cursed, and cried at me. Five years passed before Angelina was born and three more before Sophia came into the world. The girls were loving and good, and for a while, we were quite a content little family. Ursula doted on them, dressed them like dolls, and gave them all the toys they ever wanted. Whenever I advised her not to always let them have their way, she turned on me and told the girls, in my presence, that I was unjust and mean and liked the peasant children better than the right people. Hearing that, in time, the girls started avoiding me and ran to their mother for the least of my admonishments. So, the gap between my wife and daughters and me became ever wider.

"To calm my nerves, I often went down in the valley to walk around and observe my servants laboring in the fields. I liked to watch them especially in spring when the fields were sown and at harvest when they were scythed down. I liked to see how the people moved in rhythm, always singing. I enjoyed those performances much more than all the plays and dances in our mirrored halls. And so I went down often, and I sensed that they didn't mind because they greeted me kindly. They never heard me shout and boss them around as other barons did. And I was good to them. I would not let them overwork so they would be too tired to tend their own plots of land. I let them have free holidays and gave them presents on Christmas and other holy days. Ursula scolded me, but I didn't listen. She, of course, saw that after a scolding, I would saddle my horse and gallop down into the valley like the wind that couldn't be stopped.

"Well, that's the background. Now, let me tell you about your mother, my beloved, sculptured in alabaster … It was seventeen years ago, in June, at hay gathering, at the noon hour, when the air was fragrant and the sun hot. I had gone down to supervise the workers. I watched them labor and

sweat and then go down into the river to cool off. I, too, was burning up and went farther upstream, where the water bubbled over rocks, and soused my face. And that was when it happened: I looked up and I saw her floating toward me as lovely as a swan maiden. I stepped behind the bushes so she wouldn't see me, and even though I couldn't take my eyes off her, I turned away, going back up to the meadow, where my servants were getting ready to eat lunch. The women invited me to sit with them, but I hesitated because I knew it was not proper. Still, I stood there watching them spread a white cloth on the green bank and set on it loaves of brown bread, cheese, honeycombs, the first wild strawberries, and pitchers of juice. One of the women gave me a cup, and as I drank, I saw her coming up from the river smiling, her hair clinging wet around her face. I barely heard the women telling me to sit down when she came forward with a slice of bread spread with the richest butter all knew I liked. I thanked her and sat down. Embarrassed, the women glanced at me and giggled and then relaxed. We talked and joked the hour away, and then they went back to work and I to my horse. Slowly, I trotted up the road to my mansion and family. While the haying lasted, I went down every day, and every day it was the same: the girl came to me smiling, her golden hair in bright sunshine seemed like a halo, but she would always keep her distance and go sit among other women in the shadow of bird cherry bushes. But I saw how a shadow clouded her face when I rose to leave. I don't know if she sensed how much I wished I could stay and brush all her shadows away... Her name was Skaidra." "Purity," Mara injected.

"Yes, and such she was, straight out of their folk songs. Feeling love and impatience in my body, I didn't go down for several days, but then, one fine morning, as if driven, I rose early and saddled my horse and rode down into the valley, straight to her gate, and there she was in the garden clipping a rose bush. Surprised and blushing, she came toward me, brushing her hands on her apron. She picked a rosebud and, smiling, gave it to me. High on my horse, I leaned forward and took the bud and stuck it in my shirt buttonhole, but the thorn caught and stuck my finger. She saw the drop of blood and offered her handkerchief. At that, I took her hand and held it. She didn't withdraw. Oh, how I wanted to pull her up on my horse or slide down to her, but didn't. We hung as if suspended for what seemed forever, feeling our pulses beating against each other. Then Skaidrīte tried to say something but couldn't and withdrew her hand. I touched her blushing cheek and straightened up. We broke

apart when we heard her mother's call. It was an angry, commanding, and alarmed shout, and my beauty turned as if whipped and, throwing me a glance full of pain and, I thought, longing, dashed away. I was in no spirit to go home but rode around the woods like a wild man, like a thief, my heart hammering, my hands sweating.

"Finding no rest, I returned a few days later, and that was when she calmly told me that she would be married on Midsummer Night's Eve in the afternoon. She invited me to the wedding. I stood as if she had poured icy water on me and mumbled out that I couldn't do it, that it would be improper, that I didn't have time. Our eyes met, and then I asked her to come to the castle instead ... as is the custom, I said. She blushed deeper, hesitated, and then nodded ever so slightly. I rode away as on wings.

"Ursula couldn't understand why I was suddenly so joyful, so attentive even to her, letting her order new tapestries and carpets and making my laborers scrub the castle walls and floors and fix the staircase. The repairs went on all week, ending right before the longest day and shortest night of the year. Following the custom of my pagan folk, I ordered flowers to be brought into the castle. When no one was looking, I took an armful up to the turret. On my way down, I cringed when I saw Ursula standing in my way, demanding to know what was going on. Irritated, I pushed her aside and told her to leave me alone. I said I wanted to be alone so I could watch the peasant festivities down below and see to it that no one would be hurt and nothing be destroyed.

"'If that's what you'll do,' Ursula shouted, 'I'll take the girls and go to my mother's castle!'

"'By all means,' I said and helped her pack.

"When the stagecoach was beyond the hills and the sun close to setting, midsummer fires started to glow throughout the valley. Up in the turret, I stood in the open window, waiting and listening to the singing of my servants. At last, in the pale twilight, through my hand telescope, I saw Skaidra, as a bride, dressed in white with a wreath of daisies on her head, come out of her cottage. I saw the bridegroom meet her at the gate and take her hand, ready to lead her to the granary, where peasants customarily spend their wedding night. I, of course, knew that they had been married that afternoon in the little white church on the hill. I had granted a free afternoon to all my workers so they could enjoy themselves, while I, jealous and worried, stood in the turret window and heard the bells ringing. The bells still seemed to ring as I looked on, and then, unable to hold

out any longer, I pulled the window shut and stormed down the stairs. Again, I threw the saddle on my horse and went galloping through the woods. When I went back up in the turret to see what was going on, the wedding procession, like crawling ants, was entering through the garlanded arch into the cleaned-out, decorated hay barn to feast and dance.

"And then, hours later, fiercely impatient, I saw my crude plowman pull my lovely object's hand—the hand I had held in mine and still felt its beating pulse. I saw the tug-of-war, saw her resistance, and raged that he by law owned her. I couldn't hold out any longer and rushed down the stairs. I saddled my horse carefully, spreading the blanket one of my servants had woven and given to me for my twenty-first birthday—the pattern was bright with stars on a dark blue background—and jumped on my stallion's back and galloped down the slope and, to everyone's dismay, dismounted at the gate where the newlyweds still struggled. Panting like my horse, I congratulated them and then went to take the bride, who didn't cry out or kick, and set her on my horse. The crowd cursed and waved their fists. Cursing, the groom grabbed a fallen stick and came after us, but I pushed my boot into the stirrup, swung my leg over the shining black back, and, like the wind, we rode away.

"On that night, the lovely virgin Skaidra, your mother, gave herself to me— willingly and joyfully. That I want you to know, and I cherished her with all the tenderness I had saved up in my miserable union and dreams of happiness. She wept when she told me how much she loved me and how she had longed for me and how the marriage was worked out by their parents so their pieces of land put together would make both families better off and how she struggled against them but in the end gave in because there was no hope for her. Nine months later, on the morning of March 21, down in her husband's sauna, she bore a daughter whom she named Mara."

Herr Von Liebman stopped talking and kissed his daughter on the top of her head, which leaned close to his heart.

"And later? What happened later?" she asked softly.

"I suffered," he said, "and she did too. She lived with her legal husband in his hut and took care of you. Juris was a good man and never said a mean word to me, only I noticed how, whenever we met, his face turned red and his hands became fists. I didn't blame him. There were moments when I wished he would slug me, but he could do nothing. I was the master, he the slave. So, I continued to go down in the valley, ignoring the cold stares and frowns, but not very often. From my high horse, I watched your mother and you as you grew up, and sometimes, I took you up and we galloped around the field. To escape suspicion and gossip, I also gave rides to other children, which pleased them and their mothers, who gave me drinks of juice and curtsied in humble gratitude. Still, people gossiped, no doubt trying to guess what happened or what would happen next, and that reached Ursula's ears. To spite me, she made your mother her chambermaid and tormented her in any way she could."

"And me? What about me?" Mara asked, pulling away, now staring at the man who was her father as to a vile stranger, a black-masked imposter.

"You were sent to the nursery, where my girls played with you, all very amused and happy. When Ursula saw that, she dismissed your mother on the spot. But we devised a system of signals. I let her know when I was alone, and then she came up, sometimes alone and sometimes with you. Oh, how sweet those meetings were, when my *Skaidrīte* told me that she loved only me and longed for me day and night! The years went by, and you were almost four. Then, one day, I went to look for her message in the usual place and found a scrap of paper with one scribbled word: *Nē!* (She didn't know how to write.) But it was enough. I understood and leaned against an apple tree, like the orphan in your folksong, and wept.

"She stopped coming. Without giving a reason. It drove me near to madness. I went down into the valley, where I knew she would be, but when I tried to talk to her, she hid among other servants, so I gave up and assigned a new supervisor to oversee my land and my workers. Agonizing months slipped by, and then I saw her quite by chance. She was gathering strawberries in the clearing over there," he pointed. "Other women were present so we couldn't talk, but she looked up at me, and her eyes were pools of tears. She forced a smile and stood up. She was with child."

"Yours?" Mara asked.

"I didn't know. She didn't say. She didn't say a word."

"Did you ever find out?"

"No. They both died."

"How old was she when you first brought her up here?" Mara asked, noting the bite and coldness in her own voice.

Liebman hesitated and then said, "I'm not sure. Strange, but I never asked. I guess between fifteen and seventeen. No more."

"And you were over thirty," Mara said, staring at him as if she were seeing him for the first time. "My age," she sighed, leaning out of the open window, watching the midsummer fires burning below. She took the still-blooming wreath off her head and tossed it out and watched it circle and whirl in the darkness until it vanished. "That's what happened to her, my mother," she said and closed the window. She was shivering, freezing. "The peasants sing about girls losing their garlands and weeping under blooming trees and on riverbanks," she said, turning to face him. "Now I understand why my mother cried and why she made me stay with her in our dark hut. To escape the eyes and voices. Sharp, cutting, accusing eyes they must have been. The voices I heard, they still ring in my ears. They were my mother's and father's, shrill and hard, saying words that must have cut like daggers because no kind words would be said with voices like that. And papa … I saw him hit her and push her against the wall, and when I cried out, he struck me, shouting words I didn't understand, but now I can guess what they were. You, too, would know them, I'm sure." Her voice choked, and her hands covered her face. "Then she died. The baby's first cry came with her last breath."

Herr Liebman stood in the window like a statue, except for the beads of sweat on his forehead. "It was the saddest day of my life when the man you called father, mad as a bull, came up to the castle and announced that he had a son but that his mother had died. I did not dare show myself at the burial but watched the procession from my tower window. Some days later, when I heard that the baby also died, I was stunned. No one told me how or why."

"I remember." Mara went on with the story. "It happened not many days after mother was laid in the ground. Then, one morning he—you know that it was a boy, yes?— woke up screaming, perhaps hungry for mamma's milk.

"He cried all day. Granny tried to feed him, but he only screamed. Neighbor women came to help, but I hid from them. And then he stopped crying, and I fell asleep. Next thing I remember was how, again, we walked up to the graveyard behind the wagon that carried the casket. It was a little white one with gold stars. I liked the stars and didn't want them to throw dirt on them, but Granny told me to stop crying and pointed out the grave where Mommy was sleeping. It was a big grave, like a hill, still covered with flowers, and next to it was a small pit. There, men with ropes, let the pretty casket with all its golden stars slide down, and then I screamed, but Granny put her hand over my mouth and gave me flowers to throw down into the pit. The pit was deep and dark, and I would not throw the flowers down there but watched the men shovel dirt over everything. Granny held my hand so it hurt, but I pulled away and, crying, ran down and hid behind the big tree. And there you picked me up and called me *Mein Liebchen.'*

"I can still feel how tightly I wrapped my arms around you so that no one could pull me away. You carried me up to the castle, and suddenly, I had two big sisters and a new mother, and everything was bright and beautiful."

Mara had spoken in a calm, dry voice, seeing the scene with her adult eyes, pitying her little, helpless self, who, like a bug, was lifted out, as if with two fingers, from a pile of dirt and set on a rose petal, where she spread her wings and learned to dance in the sunshine. Again, she felt his arms tighten, his heart pound against her cheek, and his fingers dig into her arms as if he would never let her go. With a sudden jerk, she pulled out of the vise and looked at her father's flushed face.

Averting his eyes, she continued casually, saying, "Yes, I lived in a dream, all those years. I almost forgot my own mother and the dark hut and my papa because I pretended that you were my papa, only I was afraid to call you that because then Ursula would hit me."

"Yes, my child. And now you know why. And you know why your stepmother is still mad with jealousy—and with reason, I'll give her that much, but I won't allow her to say Hexe to you and torments you, but we both know that she will never stop until she destroys you, because she couldn't destroy your mother or her love for me and mine for her."

Mara listened, her tears of pity, outrage, sorrow, and release flowing silently against her father's heart, soaking his shirt.

"Thank you, my lord," she said at last, and, looking up, she smiled as she brushed their mutual tears away. "No matter what happened and how it all came about, I am forever glad that you are my father and not the other man."

"Oh, my dearest treasure," he spoke above her head.

"Mommy didn't like him, but she was kind even though he was mean because—I'm sure now—she was afraid of him, because long silences and secret tears always followed the shouting. When I think about my dear mommy now, I remember how she wept when she rocked me and when we walked together along the river. But I also remember how happy she was— singing, laughing, teasing—whenever we climbed up the hill to your castle. I don't think she even minded the insults of the baroness because all that mattered was that you were close by. And when the three of us were together, I pretended that I was picking flowers in paradise."

"That is where she is now," the baron said, "looking down on us."

"I couldn't understand why we stopped going to the castle then, but now I know. She was sick—maybe just brokenhearted—and wanted me always by her side. And I didn't want to run out and play with other children but wanted to come up here to the palace, where the lights were bright. Oh, how I hated our dark hut, where we all slept in one large bed like a trough, with Papa always pulling Mommy away from me and, oh …"

"Please," *Herr* Liebman interrupted, "let's let her soul rest in peace. And you, even though you are most sensitive and clever, cannot quite understand the mystery of love between a man and woman. Love cannot be arranged and ruled. Love is like a bird that wants to be free, and when it is caged, the heart breaks, the song becomes a moan in the night … So, my dearest, love wisely and listen to your heart."

"Yes, my father."

"And now I must say something that breaks my heart. I have been told that in parts of Livonia, witch hunts are on the loose again, and, I'm afraid that Ursula will bribe anyone who will witness against you. So, you must get ready for a flight. Not yet but soon. I shall be on my guard and arrange things."

"I've heard it too—in the kitchen. Because of the frost and ruined crops. One of the cooks said she saw witch spittle and ravens flying around the marketplace. She said it was a bad omen, foretelling that there will be another burning at the stake. When I laughed at that, she looked at me crossly and spit three times over her shoulder."

"Oh, how long will it be before these secretive pagans leave their superstitions behind and learn the ways of our Lord!"

"But the church made the rules about *raganas* and how they work together with the devil. The men of the cloth order the pyres."

"How do you know that? Who told you?"

Mara felt as if she were caught in a net from which only the truth might untangle her and admitted, "The old *ragana*."

"What! You've been communicating with that band of women? And behind my back?"

"Yes. Two years ago, I came upon them. That's where I learned to read and write and many other things, also that there are no such beings as witches and werewolves but distressed, mistreated, and falsely accused women for things they never did. The priests and even the nobles like you—please excuse me for saying this—set the torches to the straw. Oh, Father, when will it end? And who will stop it?"

Herr Liebman stood accused, with Mara probing his face, looking at him with glowing eyes of a *ragana*.

"Then what my wife tells me about your consorting with witches and devils is true?"

"Nothing what she says is true! Everything comes from jealousy and hate.

If there are such things as witches, then she is supreme." "Mara! I forbid you to talk like that about the baroness!"

"And I shall obey you. I won't allow my lips to say her name, but what will *you* do to stop the witch hunts besides sending me away?" The baron stood, slowly shaking his head.

"I should leave the castle," Mara sighed. "I'm like a cuckoo hatched by another bird and living in the wrong nest. So do arrange my escape, and perhaps then there will be peace. And you, my lord, go and love your wife so that she will not haunt me and make me suffer more than I do for your sins and pleasures." Her voice turned into a cry: "When should I fly away?"

"Calm down, please! Not yet. Things might not be as bad as they seem. — Now, let's go to bed."

"Good night, father."

"Forgive me, please … We came up here on this night to dream and remember but are awakened to nightmares from which there is no escape," Liebman said, taking Mara's hand. "So may God bless and protect you, but please stay out of the woods and away from them."

"I promise. Anyway, they're gone. I already warned them, and they have flown away," Mara said with a teasing, bitter laugh as she waved her hand and opened the door. "Good night, dear father," she repeated and took his outstretched hand in both of hers.

"Thank you, and please forgive me."

But with the door handle pressed down, she turned back and asked, "Whatever happened to him, my papa?"

"He left soon after the funeral, so the supervisor told me. No one knows where he went, some said to join the czar's army. Others said he went out to sea."

"Good night," she said in a cold, frightened voice.

As she was descending the dark, narrow stone steps, it came to her slowly and then with shattering force—the sin, the monstrosity of her father's lust and his shameless right to that night, to the simple plucking of the girl, her mother, like she, in her innocence, plucked the rose for him, only to wilt and die. She wondered how many other women, even those working in the kitchen, had been seduced and cast aside by much rougher and meaner men. How many of the women called *raganas* were the victims of first and other nights? At least Liebman did love his servant and mourned for her, but other men?

Sorrow for her people down in the valley—in countless valleys all over Livonia—came over her. She even pitied her crude papa, who must have been taunted and ridiculed by other peasant men, for surely, they knew. People know. Fields, woods, meadows, and walls whisper their secrets to the wind that knows no borders and has no limits. Spirit speaks to spirit and, like the Spirit of God, floats over chaos and deep waters .

"I will go down into the valley and find my grandparents," Mara vowed and went out through the back door and the gate, to where the fires still glowed and people sang and danced until the disk of a new sun rose above the woods.

***

Mara remembered how, after the many revelations and her midsummer night's wandering among her people, she walked as on hot coals, afraid that she had been seen, that her father knew everything, and the life as she had known and lived was gone forever. Without explaining, *Herr* Liebman avoided any more intimate meetings or discussions with her. She noticed that he paid closer attention to his wife and daughters, taking them along with him to Riga and other manors, where Angelina and Sophia would meet young men. This put the baroness in a better mood, especially when she put on her new gowns and hats and displayed her daughters at balls and banquets. Mara saw it all and felt more and more like the alien she was, working in the kitchen, where she told herself she really belonged. As the summer turned to autumn, her cooking and baking became better so that neither Stepmother nor her daughters, having become more bossy and self-centered, could find any real reasons for complaint and harassment but rather chose to spitefully ignore her. Outwardly, *Herr* Liebman remained reserved toward Mara and only rarely smiled at her, occasionally giving her a wink of conspiracy or sympathy, she was not sure which. She continued calling him *Herr* Liebman and "*my lord.*"

***

December in Livonia arrived in a blizzard, mixing earth with sky, blocking roads and burying the cottages down in the valley, where servants spent their short days and dark nights weaving, spinning, making ropes, repairing broken tools, carving bowls and spoons, all to the tunes of their singing and telling stories—sad stories about lost kingdoms and captured maidens and orphans. But in the manors, under hundred chandeliers with thousands of candles, celebrations went on, each baron outdoing the other, as the same guests traveled from one estate to the next. Almost daily, Stepmother ordered the kitchen servants, and Mara in particular, to bake trays of assorted pastries. All too often, she barged into the kitchen to comment and scold. Her pointed angry finger always targeted Mara, waiting for her to snap and cry. But she, sustained by dignity and truth, held her own. Her work was her shield and salvation. Each task absorbed her attention and excited her, knowing that everyone, especially her father, would be pleased. With Christmas coming and orders mounting, she and the kitchen servants had worked out a system where some cookies were baked as soon as the dough was ready, while other dough needed to rest so that the spices would soak in and hold out even into the coming year. Helped and constantly advised, Mara prepared the *piparkūkas* as her ancestors had centuries ago.

Days before Christmas, as if transfixed, she baked without rest. The magic her hands worked surprised her coworkers even more than herself, but when people openly praised not only her work but also her beauty, *Frau* Liebman, suddenly and unprovoked, shook her fists and, leaning over her, hissed, "*Du Bakkerhexe!*" She forbade her to even think about showing up at their Christmas ball to which, she announced, all the eligible lords and princes were invited to dance with their most available daughters! Seething with hatred, Stepmother forewarned Mara to stay in the kitchen that evening and make sure that the guests would not run out of sweets.

***

On Christmas Eve, at the ball, dressed in layers of taffeta and lace, *Frau* Liebman circled among her guests, introducing Angelina and Sophia and taking credit for the trays of assorted pastries that were brought up from the kitchen and passed around. While the baroness courted the important gentlemen and pressed her daughters into their arms, *Herr* Liebman stood aside nervously waiting for his chance to leave the ballroom. Startled, he heard announce the arrival of his cousin, the lord of Turaida, with his lady and their son, Prince Roland, and rushed to welcome them. Having exchanged the usual pleasantries, the elders went to mingle in with other guests, while Roland lagged behind searching the crowd and then, turning to his host, asked, "Honored lord, my dear uncle, where is the *Fräulein* Mara? I came to dance with her." The baron, holding the young man's hand in his, glanced across the room and, seeing the baroness and his daughters happily courting, said, "It appears that the *Fräulein* has left the ballroom. If you will excuse me, I shall go and find her. She will be most happy to see you, I'm sure."

Quickly, he turned and hurried down to the kitchen, but Mara was not there.

As it was already past the twenty-second hour and she had used up all the dough and pulled the last pan out of the oven and sent all that was baked upstairs, she dismissed the other bakers and sat by the fire gazing into the flames, conjuring up her deceased mother's vague image as it might now be in the dark hut, had she and the baby lived. Mara imagined her lighting candles in a small fir tree; she heard her singing sadly, looking up at the castle lights, wondering and longing, and then, perhaps, casting troubled glances at her (Mara), wondering if she, too, would be called to serve and please some master as was the custom. She imagined her baby brother, who by now would be a handsome youth but doomed to be a soldier fighting other people's battles.

After vespers, Mara imagined her troubled mother, in a simple peasant dress, put on their table a small willow basket with *piragi* and a platter with roasted peas around a pig's snout. She saw the man she called Papa, reconciled but still glum in his silence, eating, pushing the food around with his dirt-crusted hands. Later on, would come the grandparents. The candles would be lit in a small tree. They would drink warm cups of cider, open their simple presents, and then the grandparents would leave.

Papa would go to the big bed and wait, while Mara climbed the ladder up to the attic space. Mommy would clean up the kitchen, moving slowly, until Papa was asleep and then quietly climb next to him and curl up against the cold outer wall. Remembering and wishing, she would wrap her arms around herself and weep silently … But where was this papa now? Mara wondered. Was he, at this moment, lounging under a palm tree in a land where there is no snow and ice, or were his remains lying at the bottom of one of the oceans?

Remembering every word of the baron's confession and feeling the pained loneliness her parents suffered daily, Mara let her tears fall until she caught herself falling asleep. Wishing for *Herr* Liebman's embrace and best wishes, as in years past, before his confession, she rose and left the kitchen. She walked up the back stairway to her narrow chamber in the attic, unbraided her hair with tired hands, and was brushing it when the door opened and the baron entered. He put his finger to his lips and tiptoed to her side. He took her in his arms and wished her a happy Christmas, followed by "Oh, how I have missed you and how I hope you have forgiven me and once in a while say a prayer for me!" Then he told her to clean up and go to his room in the turret, where she will find her Christmas present.

"You will know what to do with it. And then come down quickly. A young man asked me if he may dance with you, and I gave my permission. He's waiting. Go to him! Be brave! And remember that I love you, as I love your mother, our guardian angel."

When he was gone, she sponged herself off, slipped into clean undergarments, and, throwing a robe over her shoulders, hurried up the stairs. In the cold room, where only a lantern glowed, she saw, all spread out on the couch, a long dress of dark crimson velvet stitched in gold. A pair of red slippers lay next to it. On the table was a fine jeweled comb. Hesitatingly, feeling all tangled up as in a dream, she put on the glorious dress, the white stockings, and red shoes—a bit too big but all right. Last, she arranged her hair in a coif and fastened it with the jeweled comb and then glanced in the small hanging mirror. Surprised and pleased with her reflection, she left the tower. The clock struck eleven as she reached the door that opened to the hallway leading to the ballroom on the lower level.

For a moment, she hesitated and then went forward, hurrying down the mirrored hallway, her reflections sliding on either side, multiplying hundreds of times until she stood at the top of the blue carpeted stairs leading into the ballroom. Excited, she searched the crowd for familiar faces and saw a young man in an army dress uniform standing at the foot of the stairs. The orchestra struck the opening chords of a waltz. She saw her father inviting his wife to the dance; she saw all the beautifully dressed young ladies and handsome gentlemen, while her stepsisters stood apart by themselves. Then she took a brave, deep breath and slowly descended the remaining stairs. Her whole being danced to the music as she recognized the young man in the uniform. He was Prince Roland, the boy who at times had visited the castle. He had played hide-and-go-seek with her and her stepsisters, until *Frau* Liebman, believing the lies her girls told about their hiding and kissing, forbade Mara to ever play with her children's friends.

Mara blinked as she tried to stop reminiscing, but her mind kept on whirling, flashing back to long-gone times and injuries. She smiled when she saw him looking up at her and extending his arm and his hand grasping her white-gloved hand.

Smiling back, in regal reserve, he bowed. Their hands clasped. She closed her eyes and allowed him to lead her onto the dance floor. When, moments later, she opened her eyes, she saw that they were the only couple left on the floor. All other guests stood at the sides, watching. In a blur, she saw the furious glances of her stepsisters and stepmother and the envious looks of other young maidens who had hoped to be courted, but they all seemed only paintings on a wall.

Suddenly, her foot slipped, and, as if awakened, she saw the envious glances cutting into her and thought she heard, "*Hexe ... Hexenkind,*" coming from the side where her stepsisters with a group of other princesses clustered in a tight circle. She glared at them and, quickly slipping out of Roland's embrace, ran back up the winding stairs and out of the bright gilded hall.

Roland started after her, but the baron, pushed by his wife, stopped him. The baroness then presented Angelina as replacement for his empty arms, but he, turning a blind eye on the whole scene, strolled off to refresh himself at the punch bowl. There, he drank and sulked until the candles and torches went out.

The next morning—Christmas morning—he stole into the kitchen and quickly squeezed in Mara's hand a golden locket. Ignoring the surprised cooks, he kissed her on the lips and, holding her close, told her that he will soon be going back to the garrison.

"I love you," he whispered. "But I will come back soon and marry you. Wait for me!" He kissed her again. "Promise?" Dazed, she promised and bestowed a warm kiss—her first—on his lips. And then he was gone. She saw him ride off down a snow-packed road.

***

After the New Year's ball and fireworks, when Mara was glad to be again back in the kitchen cooking, baking, remembering, and listening to the Livonian women telling stories about their youths, the rooms in the manor had become very quiet and dull. Snows and blizzards swirled and roared outside the windows, while the castle grounds slumbered beneath deep snowdrifts, dreaming of sunshine and spring. *Frau* Liebman was occupied in her own despondent manner, missing Angelina and Sophia, who were studying in a convent in Riga. Mara, during the cold white January, had been seen with her father only briefly and then always in the watchful presence of his wife. Since the ball, *Frau* Liebman had watched her husband's and stepdaughters' exchanged glances as too cordial and deceitful whenever they met over her head, mutely assuring solidarity, love, and sympathy. But mostly, the baron was nervous and seemed afraid.

Mara tried to find out if he was ill and sought to comfort him with a gentle touch, but he barely acknowledged her. So passed the cold, white winter months. Gradually, she understood that her father was doomed to struggle with his guilty conscience all the days of his life. Perhaps she pitied him while scorning his guilt and fear-flawed spirit, which Ursula dominated with vengeful pleasure. Naturally, Mara saw that the more he feared Ursula, the stronger she became until he seemed to crumble against the rough iron of her will. She saw that, at a whim, Stepmother laid down new rules. Now, she hackled her husband about social propriety and reminded him that their daughters came first and not his bastard. When he remained calm, she bombarded him with words: "*scoundrel ... undisciplined. . . adulterer. . . coward!*" When those brought no response, she threatened, "If you'll carry on like this, either your peasants will kill you or our governors will throw you out, and then what will become of us? You must decide on whose side you are on—God's or the devil's!" Hounded, he went riding, both he and his horse foaming, until they were exhausted. Then, like a thief, he would go to his tower room and sleep or go to his study to be alone with his alabaster Skaidra.

One fine spring morning, Mara, coming in from a walk with budding birch twigs in her hand, came face-to-face with her father at the statue, as *Frau* Liebman, walking down the hall, saw the open door and charged. Screaming, she ordered Mara to get out of the way and confronted her husband. "How long will you hide this *Hexe* under our roof?!" Then to Mara, "I know who you are and what you do, you devil's slave!"

What Mara had started doing during snowy afternoons was to go down into the village to visit her widowed grandmother, whose job was to mind the busy servants' children. She liked the children, and she was glad to help her grandmother. But not satisfied only with playing games, she decided to teach them reading, writing, and arithmetic. Also, she told them stories she had heard from the kitchen women about old times and fierce battles. Together, they sang sad songs and danced happy rounds. The children loved these classes and spread the news throughout the village so that Grandmother's small cottage buzzed like a restless beehive full of children eager to learn. Of course, that made news up in the castle and upset the baron and enraged the baroness, who, wrapped in her shawls and waving her arms, dashed about like a furious owl, ready to dig into her victim's skin. But Mara only pitied Stepmother and stayed out of the way.

But then there dawned an ominous morning, when March winds rattled the shutters and broke the branches of large trees. Mara saw Stepmother looking out, holding on to the windowsill, as if trying to push the storm away. When Mara said, "Good morning, *Mutti!*" Ursula ordered her to bring up breakfast to the parlor and go tell the baron to meet her there. Done as told, a while later, Mara, carrying a full tray, was about to open the door when she heard: "Because you have overstepped all bounds and made a spectacle of your bastard and shamed your own daughters so that no dukes or princes ever come courting, we must get rid of her! You leave me no choice, and for that, I curse you!" roared the baroness in a grating voice. "We must have a grand reception when the girls come home, and the sly *Hexe* must be out of the way. I'll see to that, and you better not try to stop me this time!"

Mara pushed the tray through the door and walked away.

***

Later on, at the beginning of May, again, dark clouds roared, bringing in rain, sleet, thunder, and rumors that witches were seen again collecting the first dandelions. As in past years, down in the valley, milkmaids again complained that the cows had stopped giving milk. Others said that they had seen witch spittle in the new grass. Mara's grandmother told her to beware.

"The eyes are on you, my child," she said. "People—we all—haven't forgotten the baron's haughty ways. They know who you are and how you came into this life and that you wander about the woods consorting with witches and evil spirits. Therefore, my dearest, don't come down here anymore—at least not until the storms blow over."

After listening to more admonitions and stories she had heard before, Mara embraced the careworn old woman and drew her close, saying, "You are the mother I never had, and I would not want any harm to come to you because of me." Then she gathered her belongings, kissed her on the cheek, and went out the door. They never saw each other again.

Later on, back at her job in the kitchen and after the clatter and noise of welcoming home Angelina and Sophia, Mara was more nervous and distressed than ever, especially when the older cook spread the news that there would soon be another splendid ball in honor of the young baronesses and that many young men would be invited.

Mara remembered her stepmother's threats and her father's warning and, finding no peace in the castle, escaped into the woods. She did not stop trudging until she reached the river, turbulent and high and impossible to cross. She saw the caves on the other side but saw no *raganas* or any other unusual apparitions. Relieved, she returned to the castle and, from then on, vowed to stay within the castle grounds. But only a short time thereafter, the kitchen women sounded another alarm: they heard that the *raganas* were indeed back and that people had even seen strange women snooping around the palace grounds. Mara laughed, saying that it's all nonsense and that she had been out walking and saw only peasant women picked flowers, but the older cook said, "Well, laugh as much as you will, but you don't know what could happen around here. I have lived long enough to see strange things and heard many cries."

The forewarning or prophecy seemed to come true sooner than expected. In mid-May, the weather—as in years past—turned cold, and a hard frost killed the early sprouts of wheat and rye. People lamented about famine and plagues and, as usual, blamed the *raganas*. The hysteria spread, and soon, the cries of bygone times were sounded again: "*Burn down the woods! Kill the witches! Catch everybody who consorts with them! Spare no one!*"

Men, even from other districts, banded together, carrying ropes and nets. And, sure enough, they found several *raganas* hiding in caves. They tied them up and dragged them away. When Mara asked where they would be taken, no one answered; instead, they eyed her suspiciously. But the answer came sooner than expected. The near and far woodlands were set on fire that raged for days, even as some people rejoiced that the land was being cleansed once again. After the fires stopped burning, people spread the news that not all *raganas* were destroyed. In fact, people gossiped that those who had escaped the fires were taking revenge upon the humans by turning into animals or invisible spirits. But some—so went the talks—posed as servants and poor orphans and tried to find hiding places in castles, manors, and barns. Ursula Liebman caught the wind of that and moved quickly. She threw out the word *Hexe* at Mara with more venom and volume than ever. The baron, as if aroused from a comatose sleep, couldn't simply ride off or hide in his tower. Frightened, he called Mara out of the kitchen and told her that the time had come for her to leave. There was no controlling Ursula, he said. "She will have no peace until you are burned or gone." Mara knew that. She embraced her father, so thin and nerve-wracked, and told him gently that it was all right. She was grown up and it was time to go out into the world, "and you must be careful and not worry about me ... but pray and wait."

That same day, she wrote a note to Roland of Turaida and asked her father to deliver it. Shedding tears, she embraced the cooks, who wished her well. She packed her clothes in a small trunk and her treasures in her large carpetbag. The next morning, in the early hours of the dawn, *Herr Von* Liebman smuggled his love child out of his castle. In the Riga harbor, he turned her over to a trustworthy captain of a ship bound for the harbor of Hamburg.

XIV

Back Into The Present

Mara rose and put a new candle in the holder and lit it. She sat up straight, concentrating. Wide-eyed—for the handwriting was hard to read—she slid her finger through the papers, slowing at the *Sch*'s and stopped when she came upon *Schrader. Schraderin.*

> *Katharina Schraderin, b. 1618, the child of a charcoal burner of Wernigerode at Harz. At age 16 was placed in the service of the Abbey at Quedlinburg, where she worked in the kitchen until 1638 … Sold Lebkuchen in the markets of southern Germany. Had a stand in the Nürenberg marketplace … There the court baker Hans Metzler noticed her and approached her concerning the secret recipe of the already famous Leb-Kuchen … She pushed him away. But Hans Metzler was a persistent suitor. Katharina fled from his persistent pressure to Weringer, but there found no peace either and escaped in the night, taking with her only her baking things. That was in the beginning of 1647.*[1]

"Ah, yes, the year I was born," Mara stopped and contemplated the meaning of that. Could it be true, she wondered against her better judgment, that *raganas,* in however many languages they were called, before they died, pass on their spirits to someone else to make sure of their immortality? Some of the Livonian kitchen women believed that, and she had scoffed at them, but now the idea frightened and amazed her. Could then this German, this Katharina, this *Bakkerhexe,* had possibly chosen her? "Could I be, in truth, a *ragana*?" She rubbed her eyes and read on:

> *She moved into a lonely house close to Engelsberg in Spessart. She bought the small house that had been empty for a long time, had it renovated and had four baking ovens built. A peaceful time followed. Hardly a month had passed before she brought to the market not only a new variation of Lebkuchen but many other pastries. Her products were much in demand and very famous between Fulda and Mainz … Her fame aroused the hatred of the Nürnberg court baker. He accused Katharine as a Hexe in court.*[2]

Mara blinked, her eyes tired and tear-soaked. "Envy. Greed. Jealousy. Hatred. Aren't they all the deadly sins?" *She vanished from sight …* "Could it have been—murder?" She searched through the papers but found nothing. Evidently, the case closed with the assumption that Katharina had simply vanished, flown to the moon on a broom handle! On the margin, some hand had noted that Katharina's story had stopped after she was dismissed as not guilty from the court.

Mara laughed cynically, staring into the bright candle flame as into a crystal ball. With that, the superstitious masses all over the civilized kingdoms of Germany were made to believe that she—this clever and successful woman —was a witch, and to defend her would be doing the devil's work. "Oh, then I am doing it! But why do I feel like I'm serving heaven?"

It was getting late, and there would be much work to do in the morning, but she couldn't stop now. She rose, stretched, and looked out of her small window. The night was bright with a nearly full moon, and the stars sparkled like scattered gold. "Witches work at night in moonlight," she said aloud, emitting notes of pained, bitter laughter. She drank a few sips of cold tea, went back to her desk, and took up the papers.

Wirkliche & akkuratateste Beschreybung der hoch Notpeinlichen Befragung der Katharina Schraderin genant die Bakkerhexe

(The True and Accurate Description of the Very Painful Interrogation of Katharina Schraderin known as Bakkerhexe) MDCLI

Katharina Schraderin, accused of witchcraft, was led out of a lonesome building and taken before the Judge Justinus Dythfurt, who asked: "Are you Katharina Schraderin, who has been accused as being a witch who practices black magic and all kinds of witchcraft?"

To that the same answers calmly: "I know that there may be witches who bewitch people and animals, but here, before your grace stands one who leads a chaste and God-fearing life."

At that Hans Sonthemyer of the Ecclesiastic Council of Lorsh states: "You lure people into the woods and for that purpose your roof is covered with pastry shingles. Also, as someone has seen, the windows are made of spun sugar."

Katharina answers without malice: "My house is no different from yours. It is made of clay and posts. The roof is made with shingles of wood. You can see it for yourself, if you're not afraid of the road."

Annoyed by her answer, Sonthemyer leads the delinquent on saying: "The witness has already accurately described you and forewarned us that we should guard against your pride and arrogance."

Katharina: "You should not listen to the Nürnberger because what he says comes from hatred."

The Judge asks angrily: "Do you deny that you bake curious pastries? He has tasted them himself. They are as sweet as the devil's excrement and as he ate them he said they put him in the arms of morpheme. He was overcome with Godless dreams and uncontrollable cravings."

The Delinquent does not let herself be hunted down and replies: "It would be nonsense to cover the roof with cookies. The first rain would wash it away, and it rains a lot in Spessert, as everyone knows."

After that the Ecclesiastic is not as sure of himself as he seems. Then Sonthemyer comes to his aid: "The witnesses said that when the people are locked up in the house, she bolts them in a stall. She punches and caresses their stomachs. Then, when they are fat enough, she bakes them and eats them up. For that purpose, she built four especially large ovens."

Katharina answers calmly: "I cannot say about the measurements of the ovens. That is the king's business."

Here also she remains steadfast: "Like the executioner knows the pressure of thumb clasps." (As a first warning the executioner shows her the torture instruments.)

The Ecclesiastic continues: "Is it true that you come from Wernigerode, or is it not from Brocken that is close by. It is said that witches dance around the mountain and meet with Succubus and engage in obscene acts. Or is it only a coincidence that you come from Brocken? Or perhaps did you fly here on a broom?"

(But as the poor creature is quiet, the executioner puts the thumb clasp on and pulls it fast.) The Maiden wonders: "Do you want to squeeze the truth out of me or will you be satisfied only when I lie?"

Katharina spends the night in jail.

The next day the interrogation becomes too ridiculous. She then swears on the Bible.

Sonthemyer insists that she should now tell how she flew here.

Katharina corrects him: "People cannot fly like birds, or bumblebees, or beadles but are forever bound to the earth. One tried it once and plunged down like that Ikarus. If the witness says he saw me flying, he lies—as about everything else he says."

Sonthemyer questioned further: "Tell us how people's meat tastes. Is it like cats' meat or partridge or the pheasant? And how is it prepared? With caraway seeds, marjory and cardamom? If not so, then is it cooked with onions?"

Katharina trembles in horror and replies: "I am ashamed of this Court. Don't you see that he who accuses me does it only to condemn me?— And you, highly educated gentlemen and doctors of divinity, believe this foolishness about cookie roofs and people's meat!"

At that the Judge had to let the Bakkerhexe go so that he would not ruin his image with the people.

That is what happened in the 29th year of the Big War.[3]

XV

Obsession

It was past midnight. Mara blew out the flickering flame. Exhausted and outraged, she fell on her knees and prayed that Lord Jesus and his Mother Mary would grant peace to her mind and body so fear and bad dreams would not disturb her soul and ruin her next day. *Amen* ... She wiped her eyes and crossed her heart to protect herself from all evil and then prepared for a good night's sleep.

But she could not sleep. The strangely conjured image of Katharina Schraderin, who had lived and baked only some twenty years ago, rose before her and would not give her peace. Katharina's soul seemed to touch her heart and beg her for justice, vengeance, and understanding. It asked to be saved from the hideous image of a crooked-nosed, gnarled, people-eating skeletal witch that was being thrust upon her by a greedy man named Hans Metzler and a throng of ignorant believers, among them supposedly also those who were regarded as wise men. Restlessly, Mara reviewed the account she had read until she dozed off into a troubled sleep. *I was young and quite beautiful and very smart and hardworking ... I feared God, and he blessed my work, but the court baker was jealous and coveted what was mine ...* She sat up, her heart pounding, her body sweating. *Was she talking to me, or was I dreaming?* She got out of bed and dressed quickly because she had overslept. She opened her shutters. She saw her apprentices coming. The sun was about to rise over the wall.

*****

Again, that day, she closed her shop early and went to the library. She returned the folder and stood at the desk facing the librarian. He took the folder but was in no hurry to replace it on his secret shelf. Instead, he peered cautiously around and, as the room was empty, admonished her once again to be careful. "Sometimes, strange things repeat themselves." The words sent shivers through her, even as the images of *Frau* Liebman and Katharina seemed to hover between them.

"Do you know more than what's written here?" she asked. "What really happened to Katharina Schraderin?"

The man shrugged his shoulders and then said under his breath, "I know nothing, but people don't disappear into the blue—not even during these dark ages. Coveting, envy, murder often go hand in hand. Money buys injustice, blackmail, and lies. People get excited but can be put down with threats, and then things are forgotten, and life goes on, and before we know it, horrible events turn into heroic legends and fairy tales for children."

So saying, he bowed formally and retreated.

As Mara made her way through the dark streets to her house, Katharina seemed to glide beside her. She walked faster, taking a shortcut, trying to confuse the sad ghost, but it would not be dismissed. *What happened to you?* Mara asked, straining against the darkness. She knew no answer would come to her from the clouds, so she turned about and went back to the library and confronted the astonished librarian once again.

"What else do you know?" she asked. "Surely you must, if you say you are enlightened and that news and gossip go through walls. How long have you been back in Fernau?"

"Six years or so. Trapped by accident like you and ..."

"Never mind about me!" Mara interrupted, irritated and impatient. "So then, if this case was well-known, you would know more about it than what was in the folder. Was there any kind of investigation?"

"The rumor was, if I can remember right, that Hans Metzler played innocent and insisted that she had bewitched the court and then flown away. When asked whether he had ever gone back to the house, he admitted that, yes, he and his sister, Greta, did go back but found nothing except ashes. And with that, the case of the *Bakkerhexe* was closed."

"So there was a sister?"

"Yes. Greta, a few years younger than he and also worked at the royal court. And that is all I know. The brother and sister continued at their jobs until Hans died about twelve or thirteen years after the trial. That's all I can tell you, so please don't bother me anymore. What is past is past, and you cannot bring it back. Life is not like a sock that you can rip out and knit again. What's gone is gone," he mumbled and turned away.

"I have more questions. One, how did you come by the papers you gave me? And, two, who wrote the comments about the trial? Do you know?"

The man was suddenly very busy, his hands shaking as he held on to the edge of the counter. When Mara wouldn't let up and when he felt her eyes probing through him, he feebly muttered, "I did … I was young then and hoped to be a writer or a detective. Witch hunts fascinated me, and crimes make good subjects for stories."

"I see," Mara let up. "We're making a story right now, aren't we?"

He eyed her sheepishly and then said, "So be careful. We don't know the end yet. And don't ask me any more questions, and please don't come back before we're noticed. All our walls have ears and eyes." At that, he turned and disappeared inside the tunnels of shelves full of lives and events long past.

But his answers and confession only excited Mara's nerves and fired up her imagination. As she increased her pace back to her house, scraps of memories crawled out of their storage cells. She remembered people in Berlin talking about the *Bakkerhexe* of Spessart whenever the subject popped up. They recalled and compared hers with other mysterious disappearances; they whispered about cannibalism in Africa and across the ocean, wondering if witches had learned such practices in some remote parts of the world as they wandered or flew around. Long ago, when Mara still sat on the baron's knee, the baron (her father), after returning from one of his trips to Germany, had talked about a witch trial and burning and that in certain kingdoms of the south decrees were passed forbidding everyone, especially children, to roam the woods because witches lived there and cooked up their magic and lured children to themselves. "Imagine such things in our time of enlightenment!" He had said that since the trial and disappearance of the *Bakkerhexe*, as the rumors had spread that she (Katharina) had consorted with the devil, like Dr. Faustus, and was roaming the earth, looking to enter another body.

The devil, so the rumors went, had endowed her with an alchemist's gift of combining ingredients that no one else could duplicate, but she, having secretly made a pact with the devil, was able to turn various elements into most delicious and tempting delicacies and so become very rich. She had sold her soul, people believed, and therefore God would punish her and send her to hell—unless some other woman would save her. The baron had laughed off such ideas, and Mara, Angelina, and Sophia had also laughed and teased each other, but *Frau* Liebman scolded the girls for laughing and said that there certainly were witches—some living in disguise among Christian people right here in

Livonia, maybe right here in their castle. The girls acted scared, but the baroness rolled her eyes and tilted her head toward little Mara, who slid off the baron's knee. The baron saw everything and forbade any more talks about witches and devils, warning, "They might well be after your souls too." At that, Ursula stuck her tongue out at him, but he put his arm around her shoulders. The Liebmans went for a walk in their rose garden, leaving all the children behind.

***

Mara pushed open her door. "So here I am—an accused *ragana, a Hexe* or whatever, full of information and knowledge like a honeybee weighed down with pollen but can do nothing about it. Not now anyway." Inside, she lit some candles and tied her apron around herself. "There's work to do," she said aloud. "And I have to do it. I must live out my fate—alone … I wish I could fly on some broomstick or magic mantel out of this stinking town and over its high wall. But I cannot. So, what must be will be."

XVI

The Season of Advent

The next morning, Mara turned her eyes toward Christmas and drew the sketches for her Advent window display. The scenes came to her quickly, and they were all about Katharina, as she imagined her tangled up in Metzler's lies:

Scene one: Summer. A forest clearing with a gingerbread house; a young woman (a witch) puts a log into an open oven. Children sit in a circle around her. They hold heart-shaped cookies. In a corner, a man and woman hide behind a tree watching.

Scene two: The man ties the witch's hands, ready to lead her away. The woman locks the children in cages. Around them hover angels with outspread icing wings.

Scene three: A church full of people, praying and weeping; a priest with a Bible.

Scene four, stage left: A large oven with an open door, red light inside; the man and woman push the witch into the oven. In her hand, she clasps a piece of paper (the recipe). Children are in cages. *Stage right*: A hunter with bow and arrow comes to the rescue. Some children have smiling faces; others are sad.

Scene five—finale: Heaven. Suspended from the ceiling is a choir of angels; below them sits Christchild on a sugar-spun cloud, and next to him kneels the woman (as in scene one, holding a golden open box; balanced on its edge is a large heart, and from it cascades down a frosted streamer with a list of cookie ingredients in pink letters. The first words are clear, but the rest blurry; the end of the streamer curls and dissolves over the tops of frosted fir trees, where the man and woman stand with arms reaching up to the streamer unable to catch it. A throng of people fill the window.

(The *finale* would remain in the window through the New Year.)

Pleased, Mara colored the sketches and numbered the main items but left other things blank for the apprentices to fill in as they imagined and being as creative as they wished.

***

End of November. The weather—blusterous and bitter cold. The day—a deep gray like an aluminum lid. The leaves lie brown and damp in the gutters. Mara watches a man raking the leaves under the naked chestnut tree. He burns them. The smell of burning, steaming leaves overpowers the usual odor coming from the *Henkers'* house. Mara, a basket hooked over her arm, steps out of her house. In a good mood, she is on her way to deliver loaves of bread to her regular clients, but as she walks past a group of women sweeping the sidewalk with twig brooms, one of them straddles her broomstick and makes a cackling noise, while the others laugh. One says, "Only a joke, *Fräulein*."

Mara barely nods and hurries on.

***

A day later, Heinrich tapped on Mara's window and entered through the cellar passage. From his first glance, she knew that big trouble was bubbling in the *Henkers'* cauldron. Heinrich could hardly pant out his warning, his fears, his dread. He had seen *Frau* Henker with Olga in their kitchen, mixing and beating dough. Through the steamed window penetrated sounds of fury. Then floured fists rose up, and a ball of dough dashed against a wall. "It looked like a mad scene on a puppet stage," Heinrich said. He had stood still and watched until Oleg came into the kitchen and opened the window to let the steam out. "I swear, I'll get the recipe!" he yelled. The words *oven … witch … burn* hit Heinrich's ears. Then the window was banged shut, and the shutters locked. "And the air stinks like a dammed-up cesspool!" Heinrich ended.

"So, what do you want me to do about it?"

"We must get out of here. We must escape somehow," Heinrich urged, freely taking her hands in his, warming them with his breath, touching them with his lips, "My lady, I'm afraid they're after you in earnest. The time has come for me to save you."

Mara gave his hands a squeeze and smiled, but only with her lips; her eyes stared vacantly as she whispered *again.* "We're going nowhere. I must hold out through the Christmas season because we have much to do." She said she could not disappoint the orphanage, the hospital, the old, and the sick that would be waiting for her cookies. She could not let blind fear drive her away. She could not allow that kind of triumph of evil over goodness. "Not at Christmastime. Not when we celebrate Christ's birthday—his bringing love and light into a world of sin and darkness … I cannot cloud the star of his nativity with our fears … I must wait and work until the holy season is over." She pulled up the distraught Heinrich, who was down on his knees, burying his face in her full skirt. "Get up!" she commanded. "If you pretend to be my knight, then don't snivel! Be a man! Be brave and clear in your reason, and don't disturb me with every wind-fallen gossip you pick up in their gutter! I have so much work to do, and I cannot let fear poison what I bake." Without another word, as if whipped, Heinrich slunk away.

***

December. A cold, dark dampness envelopes Fernau. The first snow had fallen, melted, frozen, fallen anew, powdering the streets, covering the trampled dirt, turning the town into a vision of enchantment just in time for the Advent season. The craftsmen were busy in their shops creating beautiful ornaments, toys, and all kinds of glitters for luring people to stop and look into their display windows, advertising that these could also be purchased at the much-awaited *Weinachtsmarkt.* The church bells rang, and the organ played heavenly music, making the short, dark days seem longer and brighter.

After their lessons and chores, the children played on the snowy slopes at the far end of town, next to the brewery, where a bit of woods and a hill were left as reminders of times primeval. In the early evening lamplight, they practiced carols for the Christmas pageant. Wrapped up in the magic of the season, the people seemed happy as they prepared for the coming of the Christchild and the sun's turning from polar nights toward longer, brighter days. Even the heavy city wall, snow-covered and dripping with icicles, seemed to have relinquished its might. On the top of the tower shone a mock star of Bethlehem, and people looked up to it with childlike glee.

In the bakery, work increased with each day. After Mara showed the sketches to her apprentices and set out the bowls of dough and colors, they became very excited and talked about real witches and devils that supposedly lived outside their walls in the surrounding woods—*Mutti* and *Papa* had said it was true and, therefore, it was. With fired-up imaginations, they made the witch with a horrible hook nose and large bulging eyes that seemed blind, but Mara reshaped the eyes and mouth, leaving the nose alone. Delighted, she watched one girl dress the cookie woman in a ruffled, many-colored icing skirt, like a Gypsy, while another tried to dress the man in chocolate knickerbockers like a yodeler. Paired up, the girls set the scrumptious children in the dark, mysterious cookie woods, made by the whole team. Some dared to string the treacherous branches with webs of spun sugar and raisin spiders. As the children worked, the word *Bakkerhexe*, mixed with laughter and mock terror, innocently echoed around the bakery. When the noise became too loud, Mara cupped her ears and shouted for them to be quiet. It was the only time the children heard her scold them. Scared, they saw her leaning against the wall and holding her head, trying to be calm, trying not to upset them more, but they stopped working and silently stared at her. She asked for forgiveness, saying that she had a headache. She tried to smile and compose herself and then went around the tables examining the children's work and adding some finishing touches to the figures that lay flat on the boards. She powdered the woods with powder sugar and etched the ground with strips of dark chocolate. But she could not calm down. In midafternoon, with a restless flip of her hand, she dismissed the workers, giving each a batch of cookies for their families. The girls thanked her, curtsied, and quickly left the shop. Mara blew out the candles, but the oven still glowed, casting ominous shadows all over the room.

Again, as she stared into the flames, she relived Oleg's attack and doubled over, clamped her arms around herself and moaned. She thought about her father and the big Christmas tree that would stand in the ballroom. She remembered the Christmas ball when she walked down the stairs into Roland's arms and wondered where he was now. Did he still think of her? Or was he fighting in one of the senseless battles of a war that never ended? And have Angelina and Sophia found their husbands and left their mother and father all alone in the large stone castle? Oh, how she longed for home and peace and to be out of this town, this eternal prison, and away from this Katharina Schraderin, whose ghost never left her. *Who was this Bakkerhexe?* she moaned louder. *Who was this Katharina, really? Could someone tell me the truth?* But the flames in the oven and the phantom shadows only danced mutely like distorted devils on Walpurgis Night.

The next morning, the apprentices returned to the bakery as usual. They asked *Fräulein* Mara if she was well, and when she smiled at them, they all went to work. Cheerfully, Mara thanked them for being such good artists that they had actually frightened her. At that, the children relaxed and continued to work with busy hands and in lowered voices.

***

On Christmas Eve, in the morning, when snow fell, softly frosting the whole town, and the chimes rang out gentle melodies, Olga and Oleg, all dressed in sable and sheepskin coats, pushed through the group of schoolchildren who were crowded around the bakery display window. Oleg knocked hard on the door, decorated with a pine cone and fir twig wreath. Mara came out and stood before him, herself wrapped in a dark red, white fur-edged cape.

"Yes?" she addressed her adversaries, as she stepped down with a basket full of pastries. For a moment, she stopped short when she saw how red and still festering the heart-shaped scar on Oleg's cheek was. He saw her avert her eyes and leaned forward, turning his cheek directly at her. "You," he ejected, "you have infected and branded me for life, you *Hexe*, and soon, I'll brand you!"

Mara tried to push past him, but he blocked her way, as Olga said, "Our mother orders and our father demands that you give us the sets of the display—the whole thing."

"The whole thing. Right now," confirmed Oleg.

"Oleg the Conqueror!" some boy's cracking voice shouted and fell silent.

"Who said it?" Oleg growled, glaring. "Who?"

No answer. Seconds later, the children were gone, leaving Mara and her intruders facing each other. Heinrich watched from behind the frosted chestnut tree.

"Why are you persecuting me?" Mara asked calmly. "Why do you want this thing that my hands have made?"

"There will be a feast at our house," Oleg answered kindly. "The children of our guests must have it for dessert."

"I cannot do what you ask. I have promised to give the sets to the orphanage. Their needs are much greater than yours, and they don't demand. You should know by now that I don't like to be ordered about."

"*Hexe*! How dare you talk like that to my brother!" Olga shouted and then, taking a deep breath to increase her volume, spewed out, "*Du Bakkerhexe!*"

"*Fräulein* Mara, you have just condemned yourself," Oleg said and, taking his sister's arm, left her standing in the white street dirtied by two pairs of boots.

Meanwhile, Heinrich stared at her transfixed until she moved, until she made her own footprints in the snow. He saw her—his lady, his angel— basket in hand, wind her way down the street toward the orphanage.

***

Holy Night came robed in diamonds of sparkling new snow. The organ of the church in the heart of Fernau played its glorious fugues; the choir sang, and the children performed the pageant of Christ's birth. Mara, wrapped in her red cape, sat between the mayor's wife and her daughter Johannah. As she listened to the words and music, her gaze traveled throughout the church and paused at each fresco on the stone wall: The Holy Virgin with her child in the manger; mother and child sitting on a donkey's back, while Joseph walks beside it, escaping from Herod's genocide ... She meditates on other scenes from the holy life: The *via dolorosa* ... Crucifixion ... Resurrection and the empty tomb, and then heaven, where he sits at the right hand of God.

Even God is a refugee.

"Why are you weeping?" Johannah asked in a whisper.

"Because," Mara answered, "because I pity the Son of God and love you all." After she tucked away her handkerchief and lifted her face, her eyes met Oleg's, and mad currents shook her body. She knew that he also remembered. It would always be like that whenever they met. There would be nothing else, only that evening, that scene ... He sat with his family across from her, in the richest booth. She saw the scar she had inflicted light up even though Oleg was trying to grow a beard over it. Guilty, she turned her eyes to the crucified Christ, as the priest read,

"For God so loved the world that he gave his only begotten Son ..."
The boys' choir sang, *"Gloria, glo-o-oh-oria ..."*

***

A week later, the same congregation gathered again in the same place to ring out the old and ring in the New Year. The *Henkers* were not there; they were feasting with the rich and powerful in their own bright parlor.

On Epiphany Sunday, Mara did not attend the vespers. From her window, she saw the artificial star shining for the last night on top of the tower and decided to take a chance and write a letter to her father. She knew that all letters, notes, signs of life to the outside world, were censored or burned, but she would give the letter to Heinrich, depending on him to put it in the hands of the mail carrier. The letter was short with good wishes for the coming year and hopes of seeing him soon. "I am happy and well," she finished and opened the window so she could search the skies for the North Star and fixed her eyes on that. She longed for peace and the home of her childhood, no matter how difficult her life would be there. She longed for Prince Roland and, closing the window, softly repeated her promise to love him forever. She opened the locket and, cutting a lock of her hair, put it next to the blond curl and kissed it. She would have to trust Heinrich with that also when the time came.

And now may the will of God be done; she sighed and blew out the candle. As people after vespers returned to their houses passing the shutter-closed window, they saw no shining hearts throw their soft light onto the darkness.

XVII

From The Pendulum to
The Basket

Not even a week had passed when, very late one evening, there came a loud knock on Mara's door. She did not open it but, aroused from her sleep, peered out from one of the dark shutter hearts. She saw the Henker, his wife, Olga, and Oleg. One of the Henker's henchmen carried the dreaded pendulum. She knew all was over and felt strangely relieved. She dressed herself and put on her gray cloak with a thick fur color and knelt down to pray some hasty words to the Holy Virgin. Then she opened the door and faced her enemies. Through the falling snow, she looked for Heinrich the Liberator but didn't see him. The Henker, with Oleg at his side, burst into the bakery. They clamped the pendulum around Mara's neck and stood there looking at her as though she were a lion caught in a trap. "How dare you snub me and humiliate my family? How dare you refuse to give me those things you bake and show off?" Henker raged. "Don't you know who rules this town? Don't you know that I have power over life and death? Don't you know that when I say to a man, 'Go!' he goes, and when I say 'Come!' he comes? But you, you ..."

"I neither come nor go at your command."

At that, the *Henker* locked the pendulum, nearly breaking Mara's neck. All she could see was the shining brass disk, weighing as much as a sackful of nails, pulling her to the ground.

"You spiteful *Hexe*," jeered *Frau* Henker, while Olga, Oleg, and the henchmen turned things upside down, smashing and looting whatever was in their reach. "The recipe!" cried the *Henker.* "Where is the recipe?"

Mara said nothing. When they found nothing, they cursed and swore. One mean hand gave Mara such a hard push that she would have fallen into the oven if the door had been open. She screamed and braced herself with her hands against the hot oven door. The *Henker* pulled her back by her hair. "Your hands are now no good for baking," he growled. "You must wear the pendulum until they heal." *Frau* Henker kicked the pendulum so that it rang out like an injured bell, shaking the dark stillness. Then the family marched out the door, which Oleg locked with one hard turn of the iron key.

***

When all was quiet, Heinrich found Mara. He picked her up and laid her on her bed. With the locksmith's master key, obtained with great cunning, he unlocked the pendulum and took it off her neck and laid it on the floor. Careful not to wake her up, he kissed her cheek, gazing at her sleeping face most lovingly, as warm currents flowed through him, and then, wishing he could stay with her forever, reluctantly snuck away.

The next morning, Mara awoke as from a dreadful nightmare. When she saw the pendulum beside her bed and noticed that her hands had been soused with oil, she remembered everything and knew who had saved her. She rose and tried to put her house in order. When the apprentices arrived, they saw their mistress's bandaged hands and, afraid to say anything and ask any questions, worked harder than ever. Mara smiled down on them in pained silence.

***

The celebrations of Christmas and the welcoming of the New Year having passed, the people of Fernau stayed indoors, close to their fireplaces, and worked. The spinners spun, the weavers wove, the brewers brewed, and the butchers butchered. The mayor governed. The *Henker* ruled. Mara's hands healed, and she baked.

She baked furiously, intensely, always glancing out the window with large frightened eyes. And when her apprentices also looked out, she told them to pay attention to their work in tones as sharp as January frost, tones the children rarely heard from their teacher and idol. Shamed, Mara would then drown her hands and her fears in batches of new dough and kneaded until she was too exhausted to think. She also created new recipes, mixed spices that people in their right minds would not dream of putting together, and then she gloried in unabashed pride at the results. She pressed oils and created colors she would use for frostings. The walled-in people had never seen such delicate shades of white, pink, green and, enticed, would press against the display window in awe and suspicion. Still, Mara could read on their cold lips the words *Hexe ... Bakkerhexe.* For comfort, she would then turn to her little coworkers, allowing them to sprinkle everything with their innocence. In the candle and fire-warmed shop, the mood would then become jovial as the girls laughed, sang, and told stories.

It was all a facade, Mara knew, when, frightened, she closed the shop in the evenings and pulled her cloak around her. Assured that Heinrich was always close by and had sworn that he would deliver her letter with the first trustworthy merchant who traveled north, she gained some peace. And when, one evening, Heinrich told her excitedly that the letter was on its way, so help it God, Mara wept for joy and allowed him to hold her hands longer than usual. From above, she could see her gold chain around his coarse neck and trusted that it, too, would be safe with the man who now held not only her hands but also her life at the risk of his own.

"Your hands have healed quickly," Heinrich said. "Too quickly for a human," he asserted, "and they will condemn you ... People need so little, especially when they are bored and frozen in their tracks. So— do be careful."

"You too."

The stuff she baked the next day tasted bitter—tear-flavored, imprisoned. That evening, Heinrich brought a message from his mother, who urged Mara to take Olga on as an apprentice. "For the sake of your life—and our good," Heinrich urged.

And so, come February, Olga sat with the smaller girls at the long wooden table and kneaded, rolled, and cut. But she didn't work well. She spilled things and mistook salt for sugar and cinnamon for paprika. And she smelled. Even freshly ground ginger could not cover the smell that she carried on her skin—the smell of her father's business. Olga saw her mistakes and heard the biting whispers. Still, she watched the way Mara mixed things but could never quite see and remember what the exact amounts and ingredients were. She reported to her mother how everyone kept secrets and how she had to sit all by herself with no one talking to her.

"The *Hexe* keeps her recipes hidden. She teaches me nothing but laughs at me behind my back," she complained to Mother. "They all laugh at me, especially when I spill anything. I hate them! I could kill them all!" Olga raged.

On those late winter dark evenings, Heinrich still crouched under the executioner's fogged windows like a sleuth. He saw the commotion inside but could not hear what was said until one evening, when one window was open, Olga had burned the cookies, and the *Frau* was mad:

"Get the recipes!" she yelled, hitting the smoke with a towel. "Make the *Hexe* teach you before she's gone! You and Oleg must take over! You want to be rich, don't you, you fool?" She slowed down when the smoke cleared and changed her tone: "Your father tells me that the markets are good, so we must act fast."

"But I don't like to bake!" Olga screamed back. "I hate it!"

"You stupid girl!" Mother yelled again. "Who would make you do the work? You'd only take the gold. Others will work—all those dumb girls she's teaching. What else will they do? What can they do? Your brother is clever. He is already looking for new markets." She sat down and fanned herself with a dirty rag, coughed, and, lowering her voice, continued. "The merchants who came here during the holidays are eager to sell. So get on with it! The future is yours, not mine, but you must get the recipes! And then—your father will know what to do. He knows his job, that he does, and he'll find a fitting basket, all right ... What's that? I saw a shadow cross our window. Who's out there? Who's listening?" She leaned out and peered into the darkness, but seeing nothing, beat the air with both hands.

"Heinrich, of course." Olga laughed. "He's her lover."

"Spies! There are spies all around us." The *Frau* spoke in hushed, hard tones. "Your father has been too lax. He must act now—soon." She closed the window.

***

The dreary February days passed, snow covered and monotonous. Olga learned nothing. Everyone treated her like a spy. No one talked to her; no one helped her; no one trusted her. Mara also could barely scrape up some polite words and take the girl's hands in hers and show her how to keep them from being sticky. Olga improved, and Mara relaxed, unmindful that all was reported, discussed, and deliberated at the *Henkers'* evening meal behind closed widows. Heinrich saw them talking but heard nothing.

And then, suddenly, with the bitter March winds, an influenza epidemic broke out. Many, even the doctor, died, and no one could help. When little Rita, a cheerful red-haired apprentice, lay near death, Mara could hold out no longer and revealed her art of healing, knowing full well that this would be her death sentence. She unlocked her medicine chest of all sorts of cures and preventives she had secretly gathered in the walled-in meadows of past summer days and nights, when the sun and moon were right. Now, Mara, invoking the fearless spirit of the persecuted Livonian *raganas*, went out to visit the sick. First, she healed Rita and then Gretchen and Johannah. She went from patient to patient, doing for each what she could. She cured many, but not all. Some she followed to the graveyard and then to their houses. But instead of mourning, she made the men and women scrub and disinfect, get rid of the rats, and repair the sewage drains. She started speaking up against the stench that flowed out of the *Henkers'* house and down into the moat and then on into the springs and wells. She told the mayor that the *Henker* should be held accountable for polluting the town, but the mayor only trembled and said, "But who will do it?"

Mara's eyes met Heinrich's. "You will," she said, and Heinrich, the knight, promised he would. True to his word, he began to organize a clean-up campaign that was directed against the *Henker*. This, of course, provoked a fierce reaction. No sooner had the town come out of the terror of the influenza than the terror from the *Henker* made everyone sick with fear. The lights in the tower glowed; the pendulum weighed down more women, and the torture wheel rolled over some daring young men. The rumor begun at the *Henkers'* house and spread throughout the enclosed town: "We are bewitched!"

Even the mayor's wife lamented to her circle of scared women that her good Heinrich was bewitched, as was she, as was the mayor. Suspicion rose, and people stopped loitering around the bakery window to gossip and admire the *foreigner's* art. All knew that she remained untouched only because the *Henker* was also bewitched and craved her ginger cookies. People saw that he went to the bakery himself, taking the cookies from Mara's hands as soon as they came out of the oven. "You need me, and I need you," he gloated, leaning close to Mara, breathing down her neck. Olga saw that and told her mother, whose fury burned like straw in a hot August sun. "She's bewitched my husband!" the woman screamed for all the town to hear. Then, one day, she burst into the bakery and pulled Olga out, screaming, "I won't have my daughter work for a *Hexe!*"

Olga protested, screaming back that Mara is really no witch, else why wouldn't she fly away on a broomstick? "I have almost learned the secret recipes," she said, holding on to the edge of the table.

But Mother slapped her down, yelling, "So you too are bewitched! We'll bake her instead of those poisonous cookies she feeds him!" Screaming and kicking, both went out the door.

Thereafter, the hunt to get Mara was on in full force. Fear and suspicion mounted. Whenever anything bad happened, even the good people blamed Mara. They remembered every strange detail and gossiped openly without fear of the usual hard iron punishments. They discussed in the marketplace things concerning Mara: "*Where did she come from? Who was she really?*" Some admitted to having seen her gathering herbs at midnight in midsummer, when the moon was high and full. Everyone knew that only witches did that. And why could no other women bake like she? Not even the best apprentices could repeat at home what they could easily do in the magic kitchen of the strange woman. Even if they followed memorized combinations step by step, breads and cookies did not turn out the same as with just one touch of their teacher's hand.

One Sunday afternoon, Heinrich, sitting on a park bench, saw a group of children a short distance away playing games. When one of the bigger bakery girls leaned over the smaller children, telling them what sounded like a story, he rose and, as usual, sought refuge behind a tree and listened:

"The witch magics the oven ... throws her spell on the fire, and it rises up, higher and higher, like a dragon, and then we all run and hide, but she only stretches out her hand, and the dragon slides back into the oven and sleeps, and then we put the pans in, and the dragon bakes the cookies you all eat, and she laughs and sings songs with words we don't understand. Yesss—she'sss a big old witch-ch-ch who pretends she's young and pretty … so she can eat us all … and you too." Then the girl, her eyes big and glaring, curled her back, extended her arms, curling her fingers, and leaped into the crowd of screaming children. Heinrich rushed over and pulled the girl up by her collar and told her to get lost. She spit in his face as the others ran away screaming. When he released his hand to wipe his face, the girl ran off laughing. "You're bewitched!" she yelled. Some by-passers stopped and saw Heinrich stand like a post.

Soon after this incidence, some people demanded an investigation. They looked hard at Mara and again wondered who she was and where she came from. They wondered by what magic she had undone the pendulum and why her hands had not burned raw. They were ashamed to admit that they had believed that *Christkind* had performed a miracle and saved their baker, but now, with the memories of Christmas muddled, they started doubting and looked for answers in other directions until they came to believe that Mara must have mystic powers and that she practiced black magic and consorted with the devil. Some began siding with the *Henker*, saying that the town would lose its character and wealth without the smell that sets it apart from others. They looked at Oleg's cheek with great sympathy and formed a protective circle around the twins, whom all knew from birth.

Things came to a climax about the time the first violets bloomed. At the main market in Berlin, Oleg had taken a sample of the ginger cookies for people to taste, wanting to see if there might be a market for them. A traveler from the north stopped and tasted. "Livonia," he said. "If that doesn't taste like the handwork of the Livonian women. We could get morsels like these regularly until the witch hunt a couple of years ago. After that— nothing."

They talked more openly, and Oleg asked if it could be that a young baker woman might have been accused of witchcraft and escaped. The man scratched his head, and, yes, he remembered people talking about one who escaped from Wenden shortly before an old *Hexe* was caught and burned in the marketplace. At that, Oleg described Mara and let him have the rest of the *Pfefferkuchen* and then, in gloating rage, raced his horse back to Fernau to spread the news of his discovery. He assured the mayor, the councilmen, his father, and the priest that he could prove that about two years ago, a Maria— a well-known court baker—had escaped a full-scale witch hunt that had fed many pyres in Livonia. When the mayor's wife heard that, she became so hysterical that even her daughters could not hold her down.

"Yes!" she screamed. "That woman who bakes our bread has put a curse on my only son, who now neglects his work and goes out every night to meet with her in secret passages." She ordered a mason to examine the house, and much to everyone's horror, the passage was found. A bottle of ink with her white quill were discovered, as were the ledgers, drawings, and such records as she needed for her work to run smoothly. "Decent women don't use men's tools!" she screamed. "Honest women don't run guilds! … She blinded us all!"

The mayor huffed and puffed at his pipe. But he stood up at the next town council meeting and said, "Gentlemen—*ahem*—yes, yes, seldom has there been such open agreement on one subject, but—*ahem*—we must not jump too quickly to conclusions … Let's wait and see." He proposed another meeting, where the *Bakkerhexe* would be present.

And so Mara was summoned before the judge, who sat behind a screen asking her questions. She, remembering Katharina's trial, asked, "Gentlemen, you who are smart and enlightened, how could you believe such nonsense about me? How can you be so misguided?"

"Nothing personal," the judge said. "We simply cannot take a chance and aid and abet witches."

"I am not a witch," Mara said softly. Screened off as Katharina had been from the inquisitors so no bewitching could happen, the judge could not see how beautifully she was dressed in her white costume with embroidered designs bordering the full skirt, collar, and sleeves. Her amber necklace shone from the feeble light that touched it through a dirty window.

"Then who are you?"

"I am the daughter of an antique land. I am the daughter of the northern lights."

"Only a witch would talk like that," said the judge, feeling ridiculous, wondering if he should not recall his sentence. He wondered if perhaps he was dealing with a madwoman, a demented foreigner. "*Ah, too many of them were pressing into the country these days,*" he muttered to himself. But the *Henker's* men were quicker than the judge's mind: they tied Mara's hands behind her back and led her down the dark, dreary passage to her prison cell. As in a nightmare, she heard people's voices; she heard *Frau* Henker call out, "Don't worry, me and Olga will run the bakery!"

She heard the mayor pontificate: "We must not be soft on witches, no matter how much we may be tempted. Law and order and family traditions must be guarded." She saw the mayor shaking hands with the *Henker*. Her blood drained from her face, and she slumped to the ground. She did not hear Heinrich swear, "I will save you!"

***

Mara regained consciousness when she felt herself being crunched up and packed into a tight spot. The tarred, wicker branches rubbed against her whole body. She knew she was being stuffed into the notorious hanging basket. She swooned again as she felt herself being lowered down through a hole into a black, cold, damp darkness. She came to when the basket stopped swinging. Her eyes, having slowly adjusted to the darkness, saw white dots glowing below as a dim light from above slowly circled around her. "*I am dead, yet I live,*" she murmured in dreadful wonder, trying to hold her nose from inhaling the putrid air. She was unbearably thirsty and cried out for water, but no one heard her. And then she fainted.

Time and again, for short moments, she regained consciousness from which she swooned into brightly colored hallucinations where fires burned and screaming women ran after her through burning woods. The next moment, Oleg was pushing her into rows of open ovens because she could not find a piece of paper. She cried out, scratching at her bosom, pulling off her cape, crying to leave her alone. The baron, her father, took a hold of her hand and, saying, "*Hush, hush,*" held it immobile, but she cried louder, dreaming that strange children raced all around her, grabbing, begging, pulling, pushing, baking, and burning everything to black coals. Whimpering, she slumped forward, partially conscious, aware that she was racing through kaleidoscopes of dreams and visions, feeling no sense of time, where night mixed with day, sleep with wakefulness. Wide-eyed, she only saw the black rope swinging her in stinking darkness. The stench came from rotten flesh. The glowing white spots were naked skulls. And she knew that soon, her head would be tossed down there. How will it happen? she wondered.

Who will cut off her head with the thick hair that itched and needed brushing? Certainly, it would be the *Henker,* who would do his job of slow elimination. He would strip her and scan her nakedness with his bloodshot eyes, and there, next to him, would be the hungry eyes and hands of Oleg ... The basket swayed, making small circles like a park swing, and she rocked, remembering the manor playground and the baron pushing her higher and higher, her feet kicking the leaves of the old oak tree ... Suddenly, she opened her eyes. A ray of light was passing across her; wide awake, she tried to look up but couldn't turn her neck. She cried out. She knew that somewhere up there, in some tiny room, sat the priest to whom she would have to confess—what sin, she didn't know. All she knew was that she would be pulled up and that she must endure. She must live ... *I'll see the sun one more time ... The priest will pray for my soul* ... But the ray of light vanished. Hungry and thirsty, she sank again into oblivion ... The basket swayed back and forth, back and forth ...

PART TWO

The Escape

Mara dreamed she was riding in the wind. She was leaning against a man's body. They were riding, riding through dark woods. All evil stench was gone. The air was crisp; the stars bright.

"Oh, Holy Mother of God!" she cried out and awoke.

"Hush, my lady," said a familiar voice. The arms held her tighter. "*Roland, mana mila (my love),*" she whispered, sinking deeper inside the fur collar of the man's coat as the horse galloped on. She dreamed on and then roused herself as her nerves jarred in a bottomless fall. She opened her eyes. The stars shone brightly in heaven's dome; the night was clear, the air fragrant with awakening spring. They were riding through tunnels of trees. They were galloping with the wind.

"Heinrich?" She barely breathed, trying out her voice she feared she had lost in some dark hell.

"Yes… Didn't I swear that I would save you?" The voice was proud, a man's voice, deep and sure.

"But how?"

"Later, I'll tell you all later. Keep resting. Sleep on."

The horse galloped faster. Mara felt his hot back; she saw the white puffs coming from his nostrils. She felt Heinrich's heart beating against her cheek, and she tightened her grip around him. She was a child, sick and forlorn, a lady in deepest distress saved—really saved—by her faithful knight.

***

Mara awoke with the rising sun. They rode to the edge of a village, whereupon Heinrich dismounted and walked the horse to the nearest inn. There, they rested and then went on. As soon as she recovered, Heinrich, thrilled by the adventure of having done the impossible, told her, as simply as he could, how he had rescued her. The plan had been set even before her arrest and trial. He had forewarned the priest, whom he trusted and who was the only truly bright mind in Fernau—bright enough, Heinrich said, to belong to their secret fraternity of the *Illuminati*. He was also smart enough not to let his light so shine that the *Henker* would see it and put it out. He did not believe in witchcraft and looked upon the practice of torture as a curse from hell, but he could do very little to change things because he, too, lived inside the wall and the *Henker* ruled over him. All he could do was carry the light of Christ within him. At heart, he was a Protestant and proud of being a follower of Martin Luther, whose works he read secretly and shared them with the few trustworthy young men whom he taught how to work for reform slowly but steadily so that changes would come gradually without bloodshed, without people hardly noticing them. *The way dawn breaks and turns into daylight.* In such a way, the seemingly dull priest served the closeted congregation and helped his secret followers to keep their faith. Heinrich was one of them and perhaps the most zealous and impatient.

"After you came," he confessed, "my beliefs were put to the test. It was you who made me act, not only think. It was you who showed me how not to be afraid and be ready to die for what is right and true. It was you who saved me," he confessed, holding her tightly.

"So when you were pulled up hardly alive," he spoke most tenderly, "no one woke you up for the confession. Instead, the priest, now also risking everything, poured a sleeping potion into your dry mouth, threw a blanket over the basket, and let you down through a window, beneath which I, my horse ready, received you. The same guards who had let you in were easy to bribe into silence. Poor chaps, they adored you also and felt guilty about not letting you go the morning after your strange arrival. They said they did not believe that you were a witch and were ashamed for the town and its people for doing all those dreadful things to you. They bragged how they knew what was going on in the world outside and that Fernau was hopelessly backward. I believe they dropped their swords also and escaped, but

I'm not sure. Anyway, I wish them good luck, because we all owe our lives to those brave men ... What happened to the priest and others who helped, perhaps we'll know later, perhaps never. Strange are our paths on this earth."

"Yes, indeed."

***

As the fugitives traveled farther and farther south, Mara's heart thawed, her nerves slackened, and she braced herself to tell Heinrich parts of her story:

"I was born to a Livonian woman whose wedding night the baron claimed for himself. He is my father, the one to whom I wrote the letter you delivered. He is also the one who sent me into exile. Yet I love him, for though he sinned, he was a good man and loved my mother with all his heart. That I know. I remember how he wept after she died, when he held me in his arms. He took me away from my papa—the peasant my mommy was forced to marry—from his gray hut to his bright castle. I was then four. There, the baron, my father, raised me. The man mother married, I remember as being crude and mean. I remember how dark and rough his hands were so that I didn't want him to touch me and scrape my skin with his dirty fingernails. His speech was also rough. When he lost his temper, he hit my mother and me too, but he was quiet most of the time.

"Mother, for a time, worked in the castle and read many books and showed me pretty pictures. I remember her beautiful singing voice and also her soft- spoken words—when she was happy and we were alone. She taught me many Livonian folksongs and proverbs, which I keep in my heart and which help me when I am alone and my heart aches. That was all poor mommy could give me. I now understand how lonely she was and how full of dreams, songs, and poems was her spirit. So how could an enslaved man understand such a wife? How could he understand the mysteries of the colored lights that sometimes swept across our sky? With him—the baron—Mamma could talk. They both could talk heart to heart, I'm sure, because there was no gentle talk that I ever heard come from the baroness. So, both were happy when they were alone. Even I, a small child, could feel that, and he assured me that he loved her long before she was married, while she, aware of

106

her low status, only tried to please him. It's no surprise that the baron took advantage of his rights, even though it was a sinful practice, which many brides dreaded. But God punished both. Mamma died when my brother was born. She was about twenty. . . so young, so helpless ... Oh, I don't want to talk about her! I've told you enough."

Mara rested, waiting for Heinrich to say something, but he was silent. She glanced up and saw his eyes flashing swords and looking straight ahead, his mouth tight, his arm's grip fierce. She wished she could swallow the words back into herself, but, having said that much, she had to go on and tell Heinrich about her stepmother and stepsisters and the witch hunts.

"The awareness about my mother's sad love and her low status and the baron's power and rights came to me slowly, bit by bit. I'm still trying to put it all together, as it comes to me as if in forgotten dreams and as I return to it—even from this distance ... I was only a child who, like a rabbit, jumped and played around the castle wall when my parents lay on a striped blanket inside tall grasses ... Mamma told me to go pick flowers and bring them to her only when my hands were full, and so I did. I didn't call the baron Papa but *Herr* Liebman. . . My papa was the other man down in the dark hut ... I didn't like him because he hit me, and he shouted at Mamma and forbade her to go to the castle. She cried ... She was afraid, but we had to sleep with Papa in a big bed. I remember how the fleas jumped, and Mamma put tall grasses and powders on the bed to kill them, but they still jumped. She scratched and cried, and that made me cry too.

"One day, a strange old woman came into our hut. Papa and the woman went into the room where Mamma lay in bed moaning and crying. I wanted to go to her, but Papa told me to stay away and closed the door. Mamma cried louder. And then came a very loud cry, and the strange woman came out, and I ran in and jumped on the bed, but Mamma didn't hug me. She lay very still, holding a baby who was yelling. Then Papa told me that Mamma was dead. I screamed and hit the baby because he killed my mother. He died. I don't know exactly when. No one told me, and I didn't care.

"I watched how Papa and the old woman washed my mother and wrapped her in a white sheet. He brought a casket down from the attic, and he and the woman put Mommy in it and closed the lid. Other men carried the casket into the shed and told me to stay away, but I would not listen. I sneaked back into the shed and slept on straw, next to Mamma. I cried and wouldn't eat. My grandmother came to take care of me. The next thing I remember was that our horse pulled the wagon with her in the casket up to the graveyard. All our neighbors walked behind. Granny and I also walked. She held my hand so it hurt. Papa walked in front of me, and all the people were moaning so that I started to cry very loudly. Papa told me to be quiet. And then we were up on top of the hill, where all the crosses stand in rows. I saw the men slide the casket into the ground. Granny and I threw flowers on it, and Papa threw shovels of dirt. I cried and pulled away from my grandmother's grip and ran down the hill and hid behind a tree until Papa picked me up and set me on his shoulders and took me down to our hut. I hated to be there alone with him and grandmother, who stayed by, looking after the baby. But when he died and we were again in the graveyard, and again I tried to run away, the baron picked me up and took me to the castle to live with him and his family.

"Oh," she sighed. "How I loved the hand that had saved me! How I liked to sit on the nice man's lap and listen to his talking, even though I didn't understand the words! He told me that I must forget the old words and learn new ones so that I could talk to my new mother and sisters. He gave me pretty dresses and toys and called me his princess, and I learned to dance for him—skip and whirl—until I was dizzy and fell in his arms"

"For some time, when I was little, my stepmother treated me as one of her children, but when I grew up taller and—so people said—was prettier than her daughters, she began to hate me. To get me out of her way, she put me in the servants' part of the castle and ordered me to work in the kitchen, where I learned to bake so well that the other cooks told me that I had magic in my hands."

Mara disclosed nothing more. She did not mention Roland and their secret meetings. She did not tell about the Christmas ball and Roland's kiss. She did, however, mention going to the *raganas* in the woods, who taught her to read and write, and about the *Old One,* the *vecene,* from whom she learned many things about people and life.

"I believed she was a *smart ragana*—or really just a very wise woman— who could teach me many things. And I did learn from her about herbs and how to combine and distill them into cures. I also knew that desperate mothers secretly brought their sick children to the Old

One, and she cured them. Therefore, when the witch hunts were going on, people left her alone and even protected her because they needed her. I often went with her to pick flowers and helped her sort them out. I liked being with her, and she liked me like a daughter and told me many stories and taught me many things about the power and strength not only of simple flowers most people call weeds but also about what she called the strength of the human spirit."

Mara did not tell Heinrich that because she had no mother to teach her the secrets of a woman's body, she asked the Old One, who told her how a woman's body worked and how babies were conceived and born. "The *ragana*," Mara went on, "believed that Livonia was an especially blessed place because the way the light rays cross and stream down from the sun touching the earth, charging people with waves of energy. Sadly, she didn't like the church, especially the way it made laws and allowed tortures. She was not afraid to speak her mind, even if they'd dragged her to the church and beat her. But my father, the baron, was afraid. After I told him that I was seeing the *raganas* and spending a great deal of time with them, he forbade me to go into the woods, and I, of course, obeyed and stopped visiting the Old One.

"About two years later, when I was going on seventeen, there came a hard May frost and ruined the fields. People blamed the *raganas*, as in times past, and a hunt started up again and went crazy, going on full force throughout Livonia. Then *Herr Von* Liebman, afraid for my life because his wife hated me, sent me to his cousin in Berlin. And that is how I came to Germany."

Exhausted, her body aching, she stopped talking and rested in the circle of Heinrich's arm. She closed her eyes and relived those days and remembered *Frau* Liebman, who called her *Bakkerhexe* and made her slave in the kitchen. To turn her thoughts to more pleasant moments, she recalled the Christmas Eve ball and Roland's taking her hand and dancing with her as if she were a princess who had awakened from a deep sleep. Again, she remembered their parting kiss and sat up.

"My locket. Please give it back to me." She reached inside Heinrich's shirt, touching his skin until she took a hold of the chain. She found the clasp and opened it and took the precious chain off his neck. She warmed the locket in her hand and polished it on her skirt and then fastened the chain around her neck. "It was my mother's," she lied as she kissed it. "Thank you for keeping it for me."

Mara stroked the finely engraved *R*, hoping Heinrich would not notice, but she felt his grip tighten like a hard vice. "What's the *R* for?"

"*Ragana*," she lied spitefully, suddenly angry at herself for having confessed too much. Heinrich spurred the horse, which took off in a gallop.

"So how did you come to our town? It's time I knew," Heinrich said, pulling in the reins, leaning over her so he would hear better.

"Yes. . . I left from Riga harbor on a ship that sailed to Hamburg. From there, I was taken to Berlin, to my uncle's mansion. I lived there for more than a year, but again, things went wrong. I don't know if I should tell you what happened."

"Go on, I'm not a child. Couldn't be worse than what I've already heard. I can take the truth."

"Can you really?" "Prove me!"

"Well ... All right. So—the cousin or uncle, even though his hair was gray, started paying special attention to me and would not leave me alone." Mara spoke softly, shamed by her words, feeling guilty, recalling the instances when, perhaps she had provoked that old man's lust because she was too cheerful and didn't mind doing special favors for him and his wife because they were kind and had taken her in.

"But it didn't take long before he deceived his wife right in front of her by groping his old hand over my knees under the table while we had our meals together. But that wasn't all. More often than necessary, when his wife was away, he called me to his room to adjust his pillow or massage his aching back." She paused and did not say that he had thrown her on the bed and covered her with his pipe-smelling kisses until her face burned and that she had to kick before worse things would happen. "Oh, *Tante* was such a simple woman, such a blind angel. She loved me because I freed her from all her baking chores. But this only made it easier for him to find me alone. I was afraid but could say nothing, and there was nobody who would help me, no one I could talk to, least of all his *Frau*, who catered to him like a slave and wouldn't believe any bad word I might say about him. I know she would have turned against me like *Frau* Liebman."

Heinrich's arm slid off Mara's back so that she was afraid she would slide off the horse. "What's the matter?" she asked as she grabbed the mane. "What's wrong? I thought you could take the honest truth." He sulked and spurred the horse.

"And here, all this time, I thought you were a saint, an angel sent from God, and instead, you're a ..."

"What? Say it! What am I?" "I don't know."

"Then I'll tell you. I am who I am, and I was who I was, and not you but God will judge me. It's not my fault that you made me out into something I was not! Oh, men ... How and when will you learn? How will you understand what is in a woman's heart and mind? ... And if you don't hold me, I'll fall off this horse and be a fallen woman for sure."

"Don't joke!"

"I'm not, but you interrupted my story, which I want to finish now that we've gone this far, and when I'm done, you can set me down and I'll run into the woods and hide in some cave like a regular witch."

Heinrich slowed the horse to a trot, and Mara sat up straight, leaning against the arm that pulled in the reins.

"And so," she continued, "the situation became so unbearable that I decided to leave, no matter what. I watched the sky and the birds that gave signs of what the weather would be. I baked different things to fill my bag so I'd have enough to eat and pay for my way. I cleaned the kitchen, and when the night was right, I scribbled a note to my *Tante*: '*Your husband tried to ...*' I could not finish that sentence and wrote, '*Thank you for everything ...*' Yes! Why shouldn't she know the truth and wake up? Why should I be the only one to carry her old man's sins? You tell me that!"

"I don't know what to say."

"Of course, you don't. Anyway, I packed my things and lay down on my bed and slept until the first birds woke me up as usual, and then, quiet as a mouse, I escaped out the back door. It creaked, but I ran on. It was still dark. No moon. The stars faded as the morning dawned, and the nightingales stopped singing. I remember that so clearly. They sang as if they were sad, or maybe they were telling me to be careful. By the time the sun rose, I was at a stagecoach stop. The coachman eyed me suspiciously, but I offered him some cookies and a piece of silver. That took me to the edge of Berlin. Then I had to get out and walk, not knowing where I was going. By evening, I came to the gates of Fernau. The rest you know. End of story."

***

Heinrich stopped the horse by a stream to give him a rest. Mara slid off his back. She stretched her cramped limbs, took off her shoes and stockings, and, lifting her skirt above her knees, waded into the clear, cool stream. She splashed her face and sweaty, bruised neck and watched Heinrich go behind a tree, and then she stepped out of the water to find a concealed spot for her needs. Relieved, she went to brush the horse's neck and cool it off with handfuls of water. Relaxed, she lay down in the grass and looked up at the floating clouds. "Oh, it's such a lovely day!" she spoke to the horse. "You know it is, don't you? And you're not angry with me like your master, are you?" After a short nap, she got up and poured oats in his bag and, lying down again, watched him eat until Heinrich's shadow fell over her, blocking the sun. "I forgive you," he said and handed her a small bunch of violets.

"You?" Mara laughed. "You forgive *me*? For what?" Irritated, she took the violets and tied them with a strong little stalk and pinned them in her hair. Heinrich took the bread and sausage from his saddlebag, and together, they ate in awkward silence. With sideway glances, she eyed Heinrich, thinking how much smaller he seemed next to his horse, the large trees, and wide-open spaces without any walls, without real challenges. Alone with him, now that she had fallen off his pedestal, she was afraid and wished she had not stripped herself of the mystery in which he had wrapped her like in a cocoon. She saw his confusion, saw that he, too, was all tangled up in vines and brambles. He turned away from her, grabbed a hold of the reins, and checked the horseshoes.

"Let's go on," he said and offered his hand that pushed her up.

"Where to?"

"I don't know. Let's go where the wind blows."

"You mean—without a purpose? Without any destination?"

"Why not?"

"Because I have a purpose. I have a destination."

He looked at her with silent, questioning eyes. She did not answer but wondered whether she should tell him about Katharina and her own dreams and feelings about the vanished young woman known as *Bakkerhexe*. *Should I tell him about my sense of obligation and duty to find out the real truth now that I have another chance at life and clear the poor victim's name?*

"South. Southwest. I have heard about a town called Nürnberg. It could be a busy place with a market, and perhaps we could find a bakery where I could work."

"And what will I do?"

"I don't know. Help me or do only what God tells you to do."

Temporary Refuge

They traveled for many days and weeks, watching the spring deepen in color and warmth, until they came to a small town in the kingdom of Thüringia. There, people spoke in yet another language or dialect, but it did not take long before the newcomers could understand and be understood. They took two rooms in an inn, close to the middle of town, through which ran the Nürnberg highway, connecting it to other towns and kingdoms. It was a busy place, with many travelers passing through every day. Heinrich took a job watering and harnessing travelers' horses, while Mara worked in the kitchen of a remote inn. The proprietor and his wife were progressive people, and when Mara, after being questioned, told them selected parts of her biography, they were dismayed and shook their heads in awed disbelief. The innkeeper said, "We thought those witch-hunting times were past."

But his wife rebuffed affirming: "The times of bigotry, hatred, fear, and greed never pass." She warned Mara to be careful of strangers and start looking for another place to hide. But the days passed, and by the middle of summer, they seemed settled. Katharina was gone from Mara's mind, as was the Henker and his tower.

They liked the town and its people. Instead of ominous walls, a gentle aura surrounded the town. The innkeeper's wife explained that it was the legacy of a queen of ages past. She had been very young and did not care about politics and wars but played with dolls and, in time, employed craftsmen to build dollhouses, upholsterers to make furniture, and seamstresses to sew doll clothes. The queen made room for the dollhouses and called on specialists to arrange everything realistically, as if the dolls were real people, living and working in her present kingdom. In such manner, she not only saved her subjects from poverty but also left a visible record of history.

That intrigued Mara, who enjoyed visiting the museum and studying the displays as if she were reading a history book. On Sundays, she and Heinrich went to the Protestant church in the center of town, where Mara's spirit rested and thrived as she listened to the playing of the organ and the singing of the choir. Then she was tempted to forget the world and her obligations and promises to Katharina and live out her life in this pretty town, nestled among low mountains and lazy streams. Heinrich also relaxed and stopped worrying and watching over her. He spent evenings studying and writing pamphlets against various social ills, especially about the need for public schools for boys. He hoped that one day Mara would marry him and support his great cause, but she showed no interest in his work and did not even read what he wrote. She worked in the kitchen and baked—six days a week, eight hours a day. Her hands knew no caution. The innkeeper, seeing Mara's surplus of baked goods, talked to the mayor and Heinrich, and all agreed that they should have a stand in the marketplace where, instead of baking on Saturdays, the *Bakkerin* herself would sell her goods. It would draw people; it would be good for the town. And so, on Saturdays, she became the centerpiece of town, and things went well.

But in October, when colors blazed and leaves fell, again the ghost of Katharina Schraderin suddenly started hovering over her, making her restless. Katharina often appeared in her dreams, sometimes old and gnarled, at other times enveloped in streams of light. During the days, after sleep-deprived nights, Mara was most nervous, because she imagined that people eyed her, perhaps thinking that she was indeed the old *Bakkerhexe,* who had come back to life. Especially foreboding were the Saturday morning hours, when shoppers lined up early and, whispering among themselves, cast suspicious glances at the newcomer before buying her beautifully tempting pastries. By noon, Mara breathed relieved because everything in her booth was bought up and she could leave the market. But during the week, whenever she was out and about and people greeted her, she again imagined that they looked at her suspiciously and talked among themselves in hushed tones. Heinrich also glared at her, at times accusing her of showing off too much. He said he did not like the way men crowded around and wanted to taste everything and the way women tried to copy her hairstyle. He scolded her for being too friendly. "People watch you, and gossip spreads like fumes." At that, she was angry and told him to mind his own affairs and leave her alone.

But then there came a Saturday when Mara left her booth to a helper and ran to the inn trembling in fear. She told the innkeeper's wife that some stranger did actually call her *Bakkerhexe*. The kind woman tried to calm her, saying that he, no doubt, meant it as a compliment by comparing her to the famous Katharina Schraderin—the real *Bakkerhexe*. But Mara was not comforted. She asked the good woman to tell her more, and she did, mixing hearsay with facts and wondering about *Frau* Schraderin's mysterious disappearance. "Oh, but all that happened years ago and far away from here." Still, it seemed to Mara that from then on, her fame spread with the speed of light. There were travelers who stopped at the inn only to taste her bread and pastries, especially the cookies that turned out better than in Fernau because she could obtain fresh spices from the merchants of the East. By the time the leaves had fallen and cold winds began to blow, the innkeepers, anticipating increasing numbers of visitors, enlarged the dining room and hired girls and boys to help with the baking. With the money she earned on Saturdays and from the extra sales at the inn, Mara became quite self-sufficient. During Advent, she concentrated on Christmas cookies and again created the display of the *Bakkerhexe* story, which attracted everyone's attention.

Heinrich did not like the way Mara's fame spread and was very nervous. During rush hours, he manned the booth, trying to keep her out of sight as much as possible, but as nothing unusual happened, Mara worked the booth as she pleased until one day late in December, a man claiming to be from Nürnberg asked more than the necessary questions about who the baker was. He bought up most of the spice cookies. Instantly, Heinrich knew that the friendly customer was a spy and that Mara was discovered.

"What should we do now?" Heinrich asked, turning pale.

"We must travel on. I knew that this was not the end of our journey."

And so, as soon as the holidays were over, Heinrich bought a modest coach and told the innkeepers that they must leave. The good people listened and understood. They saw how afraid Mara was.

A month later, when warmer winds thawed the countryside, Heinrich harnessed his horse, and the fugitives left town by way of an overgrown cart road.

"To Engelsberg," Mara directed after reaching the highway and showed him a map she had drawn.

"Why?" "Because."

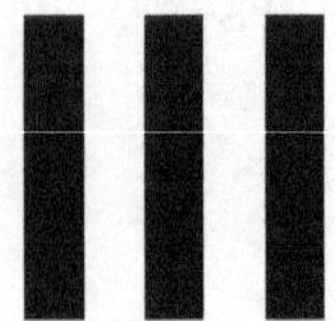

Deeper Into The Woods

They traveled southwest for many days and nights, watching the moon wax and wane. They passed through many small towns and villages and finally crossed into Bavaria. The towns and villages tried to seduce them with their charms, but Heinrich resisted and rejected Mara's pleading and complaining about being exhausted and tired of being afraid. By the time spring arrived and the country became lovelier than could be imagined, they came up against the Spessert Mountain Range and saw a road post with an arrow pointing to Engelsberg.

"Yes!" Mara exclaimed. "I like the name ... mountain of angels, not witches. Here, we shall be safe and find rest." Heinrich did not object. They stopped in a village and bought food and other supplied and then took a narrow, overgrown path up the mountain range. They rode all day, deeper and deeper inside a tunnel formed by tall trees. Heinrich was dubious, wondering why Mara insisted on going on, but she only urged him to stay the course. When night came, they stopped. Heinrich built a fire, and Mara fried sausages and potatoes. After they ate, they pitched two tents and went to sleep. The next morning, they rode on.

"Look!" Mara exclaimed. "Do you see the white bird? It's a crane, which means we're near water."

They had reached a plateau through which the horse trotted lightly, enjoying himself, until he came to a lake and stopped. Heinrich dismounted and put up his arms to receive Mara, who did not look at him but at the open vista of mountain ridges that seemed to hold up the sky. They breakfasted and cleaned up and then followed a hardly noticeable cart road around the lake and down a hill. Soon, they came to a lovely valley with a cliff marking the edge. They headed toward the cliff and found a shallow cave that would provide temporary shelter. A small, ever newborn river, barely separated from its spring, flowed through the valley, cutting its path near the cliff. Heinrich unharnessed the horse and tied it to a tree, letting him graze. He and Mara went a bit up the slope, and there, around a bend, they came upon a small house—a hut, really—with an overgrown well nearby. Still, some meters from the house, they found three mounds of stones, like ancient ruins, with iron doors and rods buried in the ground imbedded with coals and ashes."

These are her old ovens," Mara said, her heart pounding. "And look, here's another!" Under nettles and wild flowers, leveled and charred rocks mutely revealed the bygone tragedy. "We have come to the exact place," Mara said, watching the bees buzzing through the first spring flowers.

"What are you talking about?" Heinrich asked, staring at her pale face.

"Sit down," she said. "It is time I tell you." They sat down in the grass, and she revealed to him as much as she dared of her obsession regarding Katharina Schraderin, the *Bakkerhexe*.

***

"So where do we go from here?" Heinrich talked more to the grass than his lady, who sat exhausted, averting his eyes.

"We? —Well, I won't go anywhere, but you, now that you know me better, who I am and where I came from and why, you are free to leave me and find your own destiny."

"I cannot leave you here alone." Heinrich stood up and paced about. He walked from the hut to the ovens and back, examining the structure, the broken windows, and the door attached to a slanted beam with one rusted hinge. "We must rebuild, so we can have a shelter, a roof over our heads."

"No sugar-spun glass here, no gingerbread beams and cookie shingles," Mara said, trying to sound lighthearted. She stepped over the threshold and peered inside, the hut strung with intricate nets and webs holding fat black spiders hard at work. She got a twig and brushed them aside. In a corner lay a dirt-covered broom. She picked it up and cleaned it off and then began sweeping the larger room

119

and went on to the small chamber that had been a kitchen. Heinrich had found a dull, rusted shovel and cleaned it up and started scraping the layers of dirt off the floor until he hit hardwood planks. At the entry, the shovel hit metal. He picked it up. "It's a hinge," he said. "A broken hinge."

"So this Hans broke down the door and forced his way in."

"That's what it looks like."

They scraped and brushed and swept with greater urgency, hunting for the next clue and the next. At the end of the day, the floor was cleared. In the kitchen, next to the built-in small stone stove, they found a round cake pan, a rolling pin, tarnished silver knives, spoons, forks, and plates. In a corner, where four impressions gave evidence of a table, were splashes of dried bloodstains, with faded drops leading to the door. "They killed her here and dragged her outside ... so, she must be buried nearby," Mara said aghast and leaned against an aspen tree, as if wanting to blend with it, to disappear under its smooth bark.

"Time to quit mourning and start working," Heinrich roused her. "It's getting dark."

They built a fire and made supper from the provisions they had brought and then rested on out-spread blankets, discussing their options. "I shall continue where she left off," Mara said. "I'll bake, and you must go and find a market." When Heinrich's eyes seemed to say that he cannot, must not leave her alone, she told him that they needed to make a living and that her way would be the surest and quickest. "You may find a library and continue to write—until ..."

"Until?"

"Until it's over. Until my mission is fulfilled." "And when will that be?"

"I don't know. All is in the hands of God, who has guided me—us— here to this place."

"And what about me? What about us?" He took her hand. "Will you now accept my hand and my heart in holy marriage?" He raised his arms to embrace her, but she twisted out of reach.

"You know I like you. You know that I am very grateful to you, but I cannot feel what you want me to feel, so let us continue living like brother and sister as heretofore, depending on each other and helping each other. All right?"

"Then there is no hope for me?" he asked, searching for a light in her eyes. "Oh, there's always hope. One should never stop hoping, but right now, things are what they are, and we have work to do."

At that, Heinrich went to pitch a tent for himself, and Mara made up Katharina's warped bed and went to sleep.

Early the next morning, Heinrich, hardly looking at Mara, hardly saying a word, harnessed his horse and drove out of the valley, down the mountain path to find some town, some place of civilization, and came upon the town named Spessart. There, he bought as much building materials as he could fit in his coach without drawing undue attention. He explored the town, especially the marketplace, and, satisfied, started on his journey back to his secret dwelling place in the valley.

Meanwhile, Mara explored her surroundings. She found the beginning of the rivulet—a spring flowing from a sandstone rock—and drank its sweet water. She cleared a path to the well and the oven ruins. She found late berries in a clearing and picked a basketful, while cautious deer spied her from their thicket. In the evening, she bathed herself in the spring. Refreshed, she picked flowers and branches with turning leaves and decorated her new home. At last, she propped the door shut with a pole from the inside and waited.

"I am so happy," she told Heinrich late that evening as they ate supper prepared from the good things he provided.

The next morning, he began rebuilding the cottage. When at the end of the week it was finished, he went down the mountain again and returned with new materials for a second cabin. The construction took another week, and then they rested, also mending their relationship, as they explored the beauty of the woods and dales all around. The flowers and herbs and the songs of strange birds seemed to have healed his wounded heart so that in the evening, as the sun set, he looked at Mara with a spark of his former, almost gone, adoration and then politely stepped back—as her obedient servant and knight. Mara smiled down on him, and he, pleased with himself, settled into his new house. By and by, he surrounded himself with his books and took up his quill. In the evenings, by candlelight, he read and wrote. What he wrote, he did not divulge, but Mara suspected that he had made contact with the *Illuminati* and offered them his help to change the world.

During the days when he stayed in the valley, he repaired the three ovens; the fourth, they decided to leave alone. "Three is a lucky number," he told Mara, who was impatient to start baking. "But before I start, I should clean up around the other oven that, to me, looks like some giant mole mound." So saying, she took up a shovel and a rake and started sculpturing around the mound until, suddenly, the shovel stopped at something foreign.

"Come here, Heinrich!" she called alarmed. "Look!"

Trampled in the dirt was a woman's shoe, its strings rotted out.

"They carried her body and —no, no, no!" "Burned it in the oven."

"Then this is her grave ... *Disappeared without a trace ... In thin air ... Bakkerhexe.*" Mara spoke, her fists clenched, her eyes burning in anger. "They did not look! No one cared to come up here when it would have been so easy to find out what happened."

"This Hans Metzler must have been a good cook and a good baker, and the court needed him and so they protected him," Heinrich, circling the ruins, talked and pondered.

"It was much easier to close off the woods and forbid people to come here because witches supposedly lived here and ate children," Mara tuned in. "But we *will* expose the lies and find out the truth! ... You must try to find as much information as possible. I'll save all the things we're finding here, and when the time comes, we shall bring everything to light. Katharina must be vindicated!"

"When?"

"I don't know, but I will know when the time comes." "How long?"

"I don't know, I just told you! All I know is that I must start baking and you must start selling. We need money."

And so Mara started baking, and slowly, step by step, the business took off and grew. Heinrich delivered the goods to the various towns along the mountain range, always changing customers. He told no one where his goods came from and who baked them. He also admonished Mara to keep all doors locked and never talk to strangers. One day, he brought back a pair of young hunting dogs, who soon became Mara's most trusted friends.

But, of course, it was not long before people discovered the strangers. First came little dark-haired children who jabbered in their own language, strange to Mara's ears. Then their parents appeared looking for their children but actually curious about the new arrivals who changed the air in their valley. These people were small; they dressed in brightly colored pantaloons and shirts like harlequins. Every day, more and more came out into the open. Settling down in the grass across the rivulet, they stared and pointed, talking among themselves in excited tones. In turn, Mara, eager for company and fascinated by their quick movements and humor, crossed the plank and tried to talk to them. When they all had put together their word assortments, Mara learned that they were foreign workers who labored in the nearby mines.

They lived deep in the woods and were not allowed to go into town but had to stay segregated from the general population within their designated borders. By their gesticulations, they asked Mara if her man had killed anyone or stolen things, and when she, laughing, shook her head and said, "Oh, no!" they closed in around her, dancing and clapping. Excited, Mara skipped over to her cottage and brought out a basket of cookies and passed them around. The men, in turn, pulled brightly colored cups and bowls and other things from their deep pockets and gave them to her, gesturing signs of welcome and friendship. After that, they came every evening playing their lutes and singing their songs as invitation for Mara to come out. She, in turn, would bring her freshly baked goods, which they shared, as they learned about one another and watched the children splash about in the river and chase around the valley.

Mara, wanting to communicate better, began teaching the dwarfs the German language and the customs and ways of the world beyond their valley. Soon, she employed two women, no larger than normal ten-year-olds, to help her in the bakery. Heinrich, though skeptical, seemed pleased with their quick childlike movements, wit, and cunning. He also seemed pleased that Mara would be less lonesome and that the little women were teaching her new and even more exciting ways with spices, knowing that their orders would multiply. In anticipation, he built another oven and enlarged the kitchen.

"I am also very excited," Mara said encouragingly. "And, best of all, I feel safe. All my past troubles seem long gone. I cannot wait until Christmas, when we—together with our good friends—will set up the most exciting Christmas booth ever."

"Christmas is a long way off."

"Yes, I know. It's only September, but time flies. I must plan and prepare." And so she did, and time did fly. The days became shorter and nights longer and darker. During the autumn days, the skies were gray, stored with rain and drizzle that soaked the woods, which became more and more transparent. Mushrooms sprouted everywhere, and Mara, remembering how the Livonian women preserved food the woods and fields offered freely like gifts, picked and pickled the abundant varieties. Heinrich hunted, bringing home deer and rabbits; he skinned, smoked, and pickled them for storage. "We'll be safe for the winter," he said proudly after an evening meal. "Who can tell what will happen when the snow starts falling and the road closes? ... I need to buy a sleigh. That will cost."

"Yes, everything costs, and I can only do so much," Mara added, but Heinrich heard accusations and bitterness in her voice. Saddened, he noticed that his lady had become somewhat schlumpy and looked tired, as the dreary autumn days blocked out what little sun there was. Feeling helpless, he would then depart to his cabin, where he found refuge in his studies.

One evening, very distraught, he burst upon Mara. He told her that he had met an old man, a traveler who stopped at the market and bought a loaf of bread and some ginger cookies. He tasted one and then started talking, telling that he remembered eating similar cookies years ago, baked by the famous Katharina Schraderin, who had been tried for witchcraft, released, but then mysteriously disappeared "somewhere around here, but no one knows exactly where." Heinrich said he listened and asked some questions, not to appear too interested, he added, and learned that Katharina Schraderin had lived in Nürnberg and supplied the market there for some years. She had become quite rich and famous. Merchants from all around bought her goods, "but then she vanished—as we now know." Heinrich paused.

"So, now tell me what we don't know."

"That she lived here for some years and that her markets stretched from Fulda to Mainz." Heinrich paused, turning his eyes on Mara, evaluating her as from a distance. "Yes, it is indeed amazing what a woman can do all by herself."

"Yes, isn't it? And," Mara added, "as we know, the Nürnberg court, or whatever court it was, with Hans Metzler as chief cook, wanted to have her recipes, and when she would not hand them over, they killed her. So what else is new?"

"That's what the stranger wanted to know, and when I expressed wonder that people would kill for a recipe, he eyed me like I was a newborn. Of course, he said, the profits would be unimaginable, because it was not only the *Lebkuchen* but also her whole unique spread."

"And then she fled. I had not realized what a distance she traveled—all the way from Nürnberg to these mountains! That's as far as we've traveled on our escape. And still he found her." Mara sat thinking, looking out of the window, which the rain streaked in steady streams. "Oleg might also find me and kill me," she said softly.

"Yes, and that is why I don't want you to go anywhere. It is a very mean world out there," he said. "You draw attention to yourself, and people talk. News travels."

"Still, I want to get out," she said, her temper flaring like lightning, shooting bolts of anger. "Am I to be a prisoner forever in this valley, these fields like paradise you created for me? I need to get out and feel the beat of life. I want to live, don't you know? I'm tired of your watching me, guarding my every move … I'd rather die than suffocate in this fenced-in pasture!"

She burst into tears, clenching her fists, charging at Heinrich, telling him to stop judging her and looking at her with his sad, yearning eyes. "You choke me! You shackle me!" She cried and heaved until she fell on her bed exhausted, clutching at her hidden locket. "You see, I've turned wild," she whispered and wept on silently. "I've drawn all my strength out of my spirit. It's nothing but a dry well. It's empty, and I need to fill it—with people and new life. And I'm sick of living with the ghost of the witch! I must go to town once in a while—if only to church on Sundays."

Heinrich stared at her as if seeing her for the first time. "Perhaps you are …"

"… a witch!" shouted Mara, rising. "Go on and say it! Say the word. *Hexe —Bakkerhexe!*" And then she laughed, a mean, sarcastic laugh that hurt Heinrich's ears. He left her alone and went to take care of the dogs, who howled and whined outside.

"Men!" Mara watched him. "When will they ever learn? When will they understand?"

The very next day, a sunny autumn day, Mara insisted on going with Heinrich. They rode into a small, cozy town, nestled with its back against the mountain range. While he bargained, she walked around the shops and bought clothes, dishes, and books. On their way back to the valley, she was jovial. Her face glowed with excitement as she measured the distance and the length of time it would take her to make a round trip to town and back. It could be done, though she would have to walk fast. She spotted a narrow, overgrown footpath that promised a shortcut out. She did not tell Heinrich about that. The mere chance, the possibility of having her own secret gateway to freedom, put a sprint in her step and a glow on her cheek. Even the dwarf women noticed the change and told her that she was beautiful, especially in her new cloak she had made. Thereafter, she ventured out whenever Heinrich left early and would return late or the next day, and with each venture, she became bolder, even careless, so that people noticed her and said words to her, but she barely lifted her eyes and quickly slid away.

Then at the *Oktoberfest*, while she again browsed around the marketplace, she thought she recognized a familiar face, a young face that looked old, like a mask. For a moment, Mara stared at the figure intensely, and through the apparitions' rimmed spectacles, she spied a pair of bright eyes staring back at her in unguarded surprise. *Could it really be who I think it is? Trudi? The mousy Fernau mayor's servant? But it could not be. She could not have aged that much in a year …* Frightened, Mara lost herself in the crowd and found the coach that took her to the crossing where she had to get out and walk the rest of the way back to the valley. She made some casual loops until she came upon her secret path up the mountain.

Mara did not mention the encounter to Heinrich when he came home in the evening, nor did he notice anything unusual. In the morning, she helped him load the wagon, acting cheerfully, but as soon as he was gone and she started working, her hands shook and things fell on the floor. To compose herself, she went for a walk while the dough was rising and returned somewhat calmed, with a full basket of mushrooms.

Mindful of the quietness of the autumn day, she sat down on a mossy stump and started to clean her harvest when, looking up, she noticed a magpie pecking and pulling at a twig with a kind of funny seriousness. She walked up to the tree and looked up and saw that the bird was actually pulling at a string. *Strange,* she thought. *Why would a string be up in a tree?* Curious, she waited for the evening when the elves would come home from their mines or wood clearing. She then raced across the valley to find the most agile one and asked him to climb up the tall tree and find out what was at the end of the mysterious string. She stood below and watched the elf pound and chisel and, at last, come down with a piece of paper at the end of the faded string. Proudly, he gave it to her. Mara thanked him with a loaf of bread and told him to be off.

Left alone, she unfolded the weather-beaten paper with trembling hands and saw at the top underlined the word *Lebkuchen*. *"It is the secret recipe!"* she whispered in wonder as if she had found the Holy Grail. She squinted, trying to decipher every letter, every word, written with a hard-to-read but neat hand. To her disappointment, Katharina had listed only the ingredients without any further directions. Mara sat holding the paper close to her heart, imagining how *the witch* must have mixed and measured, rolled, and arranged the cookies on her large pans; she imagined the texture and the fragrance as they came out of the oven and then the loaded cart rolling down the hill, going to the market. Excited, Mara knew exactly what to do. She copied the ingredients and then folded up the original. She understood that Katharina had hidden the recipe from Hans and Greta, perhaps writing it in a hurry, cutting quickly into the sapling oak tree, glancing over her shoulder as she saw her pursuers coming nearer and nearer ...

Mara pondered her imagined scenario, feeling her heartbeat, feeling as if someone were after her and reviewed her encounter with Trudi.

At any rate, Katharina had hidden the coveted recipe so someone would find it, Mara was now sure of that. *But did she foresee that I would be the one? Am I responsible for keeping her secret?* She wondered and tied a new string to it. The next day, she found the same elf and asked him to climb back up the tree and put the piece of paper back where he had found it and seal up the cut. *If I don't succeed in exposing the murder of Katharina, someone else might.* She looked up at the nearly bare tree that seemed to poke its branches right into the sky. *You will guard our secret, I trust*, she breathed into the swaying branches and put her arms around the gnarled trunk, feeling serene joy and peace.

When Heinrich made the next trip to the market with the cartful of her goods, Mara casually asked him to buy for her the ingredients on her list. When he, sensing her feigned calmness, asked for an explanation, she scowled and said, "Please don't always ask so many questions. I know what I am doing."

Ever since her outburst, Heinrich was changed, becoming more cautious, more observant and distrustful of *his lady*. She, in turn, was fully aware that she had dashed what was left of his image of her as a saint and gradually, painfully replaced it with another: a smart and resourceful but dangerous woman who brought in money for both. Now, his look of distrust told her that he might think her insane, mad, and unpredictable. She, of course, knew that out in the marketplaces were other girls and young women on the lookout for husbands, no doubt flirting and enticing her obedient, neglected mate and would be more than glad to embrace him. *And then what would I do? What would I ever do without my faithful knight?* At that thought, she smiled and said, "If the recipe I have in mind works, we both will profit greatly. So trust me, and good luck!" She kissed his cheek. "I shall wait up for you," she assured him and pressed his hand warmly.

But as soon as his wagon disappeared among the barren trees, her mask fell off. She was afraid, knowing very well that if she were discovered, they would have to flee again, and she would have to depend on him until they found another hiding place and then go on and on and so on. The thought of another escape frightened her. She could not imagine riding on the same horse with him, leaning against him, being dependent on him. *No, never! I could not!* She, for the first time, contemplated running away, telling herself that she was disgusted, repulsed by his brooding and demanding she bake more and even accusing her of being careless; the crusts, he recently said, were too hard, the bottoms were burned, and people complained. She listened but didn't believe him because her breads certainly were not burned. *It's you who are burned,* she thought and understood that without his ideals, centered on her so dramatically and for so long, he had lost his purpose in life and was running errands, going back and forth without any nobility or a higher goal. He had become a little man, a mere merchant, her servant, even slave. She saw that he was putting on weight, that all he worried about was the money he counted every night by his candle's dim flame. But the coins he counted never reached his expectations. There was never enough money for a sleigh—a good one—and they needed the money for the sleigh before deeper snowfalls covered the roads. She did not tell him that she kept a part of their income in a chest buried in the ground against the fateful hour when she would be left alone. *And Roland?* She opened the locket and put his hair against her lips and closed her eyes. *Does he still think of me? Are we still bound by our quick promises?*

The next time she went into town, she took her chance and posted a letter to Livonia, to the castle of Wenden, to *Herr Von Liebman,* with a note inside for Prince Roland. As the letter slipped from her hand, she wordlessly asked Holy Mary's forgiveness for deceiving Heinrich, who had forbidden her to go anywhere without his permission. *But love excuses many sins,* she convinced herself and clutched her locket.

IV

Meanwhile in Fernau

The mayor, the Henker, and other citizens hungered for Mara's cookies. Everyone except the Henkers repented their treatment of her. *Frau* Henker, who had taken over the bakery, had not given up on Olga. She made her bake and bake until the bread came out quite well. Also, she kept some of the better apprentices and forced them to remember the *Bakkerhexe's* secrets and try, try, try again. Of course, the people bought whatever was available, praising the baking girls, as their taste buds, dulled with saliva, forgot the pure, clean taste.

When fame about Olga's unusual baked goods started spreading over the town's high walls, *Frau* Henker wanted Mara's recipes with insatiable greed. She heard that all around, the markets were booming; women baked less at home and shopped more.

"Much of what's sold out there is nothing special. Olga can bake better than that, and whoever these bakers are, they are making money and getting rich, while we struggle inside our walls and get nowhere. We deserve to be rich like everyone else ... So, my husband, something should be done about it and as quickly as possible. Your adorable *Bakkerhexe* is gone, who knows where, perhaps to America, but there are others."

In fact, she heard somehow—perhaps from the south wind—that down in the Kingdom of Hesse, close to the Spessart Mountains, some strangers were selling unheard-of delicacies and decided to send spies out to see what was going on in the world—what was in demand and what sold best. Not bothering her husband, she had hired a driver and persuaded the mayor's underpaid and overworked servant Trudi to go and explore, promising a handful of gold as a reward. She showed Trudi how to make herself up to look like an old woman and charged her to look sharp and make a report. The preparations done, she gave her spy a pouch full of coins and containers of food, made her comfortable in the coach, and opened the heavy gate herself.

When, a month later, Trudi returned with a carefully drawn map of the place she had surveyed and samples of various pastries, *Frau* Henker was very excited and talked to her husband and children about expanding their business and opening outlets in other kingdoms beyond the wall. Olga and Oleg agreed it should be done quickly, but they needed new recipes, which the girl had not brought back. *Frau* Henker scolded Trudi for being stupid and asked her how and where the best places would be for them to open new shops. Sly Trudy, seeing a way out of the mayor's servitude, grinned and said that she had found just the right place and could tell Oleg where it was. "And I found something else," she teased, "something that would make your blood boil." *Frau* Henker grabbed her by the shoulders and shook her, trying to shake out her secret. "Not without the reward you promised," Trudi said, pulling herself free. They argued and bargained, and at last, *Frau* Henker decided to pay her with three pieces of real gold and went to pull them from her secret hiding place.

"You promised a handful."

The *Frau* wrapped her fingers around the money and said, "See, my hand is full. Now tell me!"

"Put them in my hand, only then I'll talk."

"You slut!" *Frau* Henker shouted but shoved the gold in the course outstretched hand.

Then Trudi spoke. "I saw *Fräulein* Mara, the *Bakkerhexe,* in Schönberg. There, people are cultured and have refined tastes. They buy only what's best, and, therefore, I doubt if they'd buy anything that you and Olga make, if you don't mind my saying so. You know yourself that there's no better baker in the world than beautiful and clever *Fräulein* Mara—who is now even prettier than when she lived in this stinking town."

Frau Henker's face turned red. She ordered Trudi to scat and keep her mouth shut. She told her husband the news, and, of course, the *Henker* promised to help find the lost *Hexe* by whatever means it would take.

In mid-November, they sent Trudi back to the Spessart Mountains with a pair of real spies. "Go!" *Frau* Henker commanded. "And find out exactly where she lives, where she bakes and sells her goods, even if you have to go through seven kingdoms and walk across seven mountains and rivers. But don't talk to her, don't let her know who you are, and don't come back until you have found out in what cave she hides. And—you know what will happen to you if you try to escape!"

The spies knew. Everybody knew. Hardly anyone in Fernau died a natural death—except when a plague would strike. The town's register showed the dates of deaths: they hung in clusters. *So many and so young,* a stranger might moan and wonder. Terror perpetrated by the Henkers had actually increased, since Oleg was surpassing his father in cruelty and *Frau* Henker and Olga were keen on reporting any discontent or comments that escaped the careless lips of young bakers.

Ever since Heinrich's rescue of Mara, the old guards were gone and new ones put in their place. The old keys were replaced by new ones, and the spy system was tightened. The church was closed except for Sunday worship hours, when spies sat among the congregation. The young librarian was put in prison, and another man minded the desk and watched who came in and who went out. Everybody was paired up, and all had to report any irregularities to the town council, which the *Henker* ruled like a deranged king, while *Frau* Mayor went about lamenting for her son, crying that he was bewitched and only *she* knew where he was. The mayor also mourned and tried to trace his son's steps but failed. His inquiries and secret messages irritated the *Henker,* who replaced the mayor with a hard black-bearded man who spoke German with a heavy accent and hated Germans. He swore allegiance to the executioner. In such manner, the town was brought quickly to order. The new mayor agreed that *the witch* must be found and brought back with her recipes so that the bakery exports could get started. And, naturally, that whole prospect—suddenly brought out in the open—awakened *Herr* Henker's craving for Mara's gingerbread, even though he said that he had become quite satisfied with his daughter's products. At times, he even praised her, saying, "Imitation is also an art."

"But now we must have the real thing!" shouted *Frau* Henker, impatient for the spies to return.

***

While all that was going on in Fernau, the spies traveled over mountains and rivers, through rain, slush, and sunshine, until they crossed the Spessart Mountain Range and scouted around the small-town markets looking for clues and asking questions. At last, by mid-December, they came upon the River Fulda and crossed over into town. They found the marketplace in the center of town through which ran a wide road with signposts pointing south to Nürnberg and north to Kassel. "It's a commercial center. We should find something here," one spy said to the other and went looking for a pastry and bread stand, stopping at other vendors, and being especially attracted to the small people dressed in colorful costumes. Some sold painted toys, while others danced and did acrobatics to the tunes of strange musical instruments. At last, they spotted a booth where the baked goods were sold and around which crowded more people than at other booths. For a moment, the spies stood amazed at the variety and aroma and then pushed themselves closer to the counter and started sampling. When they lingered, unable to decide what to buy, a stocky bearded man who managed the market stepped forward and offered the strangers a sample of "our newly discovered *Lebkuchen* from a secret recipe." The spies took samples but could not decide whether they liked the strange taste. They asked what the ingredients were, but the vendor brushed them off, saying it was a secret not to be divulged and told them to please move on and make room for others. Annoyed, the spies bought the whole large container, the size of a pail, and left as if their feet were on fire.

They arrived in Fernau a day before Christmas and presented their find to the *Henker*. He ate, smacking his lips, saying it was not exactly what he expected, not what he remembered *his* witch had baked. At that, the spies gave him a smaller box of ginger cookies. "Yes!" *Herr Henker* shouted. "Yes, yes!" he called out as he gorged himself. "The recipe! Where is it?"

The spies, nervously fidgeting, admitted that they had not been able to get it. "We never saw the *Bakkerhexe*. No one would answer our questions. When we insisted, the man shouted for us to go away, saying it was his property, or he'd call the police, and so we bought what was there and left. We asked other vendors, but no one would tell us where the baker lived. One older woman said that whoever she was and wherever she lived was good for their market, and no one wants any harm to come to her *like it did to the other.*" The spies described the mountains and the treacherous roads, the lakes and rivers they crossed as they searched the woods but found nothing.

"You fools!" *Frau* Henker shouted, her blood pressure sky-high. "Why didn't you bribe the man who minded the booth? Why didn't you put a knife to his back and make him take you to the *Bakkerhexe?*" When the spies stammered, trembling in fear, the *Frau* said, "You failed and deserve to be punished. It's up to my *Herr* what he'll do with you … Get out of my sight!" she screamed. When they were gone, she said to herself, "I'll talk to my Oleg. He'll find her."

That evening, at the supper table, no sooner had Mara's name been spoken than Oleg's scar turned purple red. His mother saw it. "Ah, it hasn't died, the thing that binds you … So, my son, you must go to her. Get the recipe even if you have to kill her."

"Yes … But we'll do it after winter is over … in the spring, when it will be more pleasant, let's say in the month of May, when she would be out sunning herself or picking flowers. Olga must come with me. We'll have a most pleasant excursion."

V

Final Confrontation

In the following month of May, Oleg and Olga, having armed and made themselves comfortable in a two-horse coach, set out into the wide world. They followed the map the spies had drawn until, by June, they arrived at an inn in Aschaffenburg, at the foothills of the Spessart Mountain Range. There they found an inn with a talkative host and hostess. Oleg told them that they were on some secret state mission, but, first, they wanted to explore the close-by woods and countryside. The innkeepers made suggestions and also warned them not to go deeply into the *Hexenwald* because, lately, people have been spreading rumors, saying that witches had been seen roaming round about. At that, the brother and sister winked at each other. The next morning, dressed in local peasant garb, they rode into the woods on a stone- paved, overgrown path, as instructed. At the end of the day, at sunset, they arrived at the edge of the same lake as Mara and Heinrich had a year before and saw the same white birds flying over the waters.

"Witches always live near water," Olga said, gloating, hugging her brother. As twilight deepened, they drove off the path, farther into the woods. They unharnessed the horses, made a fire, ate what they had brought along, and prepared to spend the night sleeping in the coach, as usual. In the morning, they were awakened by a distant clip-clop of horse's hoofs. They disembarked, quickly filled the bags with oats to keep the horses quiet, and, hiding in the underbrush, went up close to the road. Stealthily, they waited for the driver to pass.

"It's Heinrich!" Oleg said, ready to leap forward, his hand on his sheath, but Olga stopped him. "Wait! We'll get him later, the traitor!"

Oleg stood up, releasing the handle of the dagger. "All right. At least we know we're on the right track, and he'll be out of our way. I was worried about that."

"Let's go now and surprise the witch!" Olga urged, skipping back to the coach, picking up a rope and a kerchief. They watered the horses, tied them up, and started on their descent on foot. They followed an obscure path rounding the lake and climbed a cliff. From there, they saw the whole valley edged by the other mountain range. Directly below, above some bushes, three thin smoke stacks were rising straight up like God-accepted offering.

"Looks like she's getting ready to bake," Olga said. "But she won't get to taste any of it." She laughed, jumping up and down, holding on to her brother's hand.

They crept along the ridge until they spied two cottages near a stream. With his spyglass, Oleg drew the scene close to his eyes and soon saw Mara coming out of the larger cottage. They saw two hounds spring up, romping around their mistress, as she picked up some logs from a wood pile and carried them to the ovens. Olga impatiently grabbed the binocular. "Yes, that's her for sure!" Not quite believing their good luck, they clasped hands and waited, watching Mara feed the dogs and then go inside. They did not see the two dwarf women in the kitchen kneading dough and greasing pans. Suddenly, the dogs barked.

"There's your problem," Olga said.

"Nonsense." Oleg pulled the dagger from his shield. "I'll handle them easy."

As if hearing him, the dogs barked louder. Mara appeared in the doorway. Oleg took up the spyglass and focused on his object. Memories, impressions, desire, and fury rushed through his being and in beads of sweat gathered on his forehead. His heart raced, eager to carry out its mission. Again, the dogs gave out sharp barks, but Mara muzzled them with her hands and then went back inside.

Olga pulled her brother's arm. "Let's go," she urged. "Now's the time. You take care of the dogs."

They stole cautiously down the path without stirring a branch, but the dogs picked up the vibrations and strange scent and rushed forward, all of a sudden barking furiously, racing up the rocky path. Baring their teeth and growling, they jumped for Oleg's chest. He speared them quickly, one after the other, and, blood-splattered though he was, hurried on and came face-to-face with Mara, who was running after the dogs. Recognizing her old adversaries, she stopped short.

"You!" she said, looking hard at brother and sister.

"Good morning," Oleg bowed, grinning. "So, we meet again."

"You didn't think we'd find you," Olga added. "But we did."

"You killed my dogs, you beasts!" Mara shouted, staring at the splattered blood all over Oleg's chest. "Go wash yourselves off, if you can, my friends!" She pointed to the stream. I'll get the towels."

"And then will you invite us in and offer some refreshment—nice and polite."

"If you behave," Mara said calmly. "I'll go and set the table." She hurried inside, bumping into her two helpers, pushing them back, telling them to get out the back door and run for help.

Meanwhile, Oleg had gone to the rivulet and taken off his shirt, exposing his black-haired chest and large muscles for Mara to see. Then both brother and sister took their time washing themselves and, Mara surmised, talking over their strategy. She also wondered how to proceed—fight or comply? Scream (but who would hear her?) or quietly follow orders? She found no answer, no clue, before Oleg called for the towels. She stepped forward and tossed them. Oleg caught one, laughing, facing her, rubbing his chest. "Glad to see me?" He saw her hesitate and look down. "You like me, don't you? I've grown up. A real man, like you need, not that idiot you're with. You married or what? Living like a whore or a Gypsy all by yourself, aren't you?" "Think you could get away," Olga added. "Think there's no spies or police that can find you and give you what you deserve, both of you—traitors and thieves!"

"Shut up! Let's not forget our manners, like Mamma taught us … Didn't your witch's nose tell you that we were hunting for you these many days?"

"Yes, I knew you'd come sooner or later."

"Well, then, here we are, your long-awaited guests. Let's go into your castle," Oleg said, bowing, and pushed his way through the door. Olga followed. Mara, still trying to assess the situation, slowly set out a loaf of bread and a pitcher of juice and sat down. Calmly, she eyed both and inquired about Fernau, about the mayor's family—for Heinrich's sake, she added. She asked about those who had worked for her and, at last, about their parents. "How is your father? Is he well? Does he get what he wants?"

She was stretching out time, hoping to avoid enraging the pair, as she nervously glanced out the window and spotted the dwarf women moving fast at the far side of the meadow.

"All right, all right," Oleg said and cut another chunk of bread. "All's fine. The wall is easier to escape now, and people do, but when they're caught, they have to deal with my father. You, too, will have to face him—both of you. You have committed high treason. You will hang again in the basket— unless you give us your famous recipes— *Ach*, don't act innocent! We know you are the mysterious *Bakkerhexe* everyone is talking about, so you better be good to us, and we'll save your pretty skin."

"I am now good to you, am I not?"

"Not enough. We didn't tramp all this way to discuss history and politics."

"But I'm most interested," Mara said, trying to drag out the conversation, keeping her nerves calm, trying to listen what was said and glancing out the lace-curtained window. Suddenly, startling the twins, she sprang to her feet as she spied six moving figures far at the edge of the valley.

"Why did you jump up? Who's out there?"

"Nobody. The deer come down to the stream. But, friends, I have work to do. The dough is rising."

"So it is!" Oleg laughed and ran his hand up and over her chest.

She pushed it away, shouting, "Go on with it! Tell me what you want and then go! Get out!" She bolted for the door, but he pulled her back.

"You know why we came," Olga answered for her brother. "We want your *Lebkuchen* and ginger cookie recipes and whatever else you have."

"Why?"

"You stupid witch, don't you know what's going on in the world? People are breaking into big markets, outdoing each other, getting rich, but what they're selling is nothing special. We want to outdo them. So, we want your recipe. Doesn't that make you proud? ... We'll even pay for it. Mamma gave me a gold piece for you. Fair is fair, she said," Olga bargained like a businesswoman.

"I don't have any recipes you could read and follow."

"Don't lie, you witch!" Olga screamed. "We know you bake *Lebkuchen*. So you must have the old recipe from the old *Bakkerhexe*. That's what the old people back home say. They say another witch is baking the real thing. So give it to me!"

"No."

"No!" Oleg squeezed her hand so her knuckles cracked. "You dare say that? Again? And here we've been all nice and talking like old friends. Go away, Olga! I need to talk to our *Bakkerhexe* in private."

As soon as Olga was out the door, he pulled Mara up against him, devouring her face with his hungry mouth, panting, and sweating. He ripped off her apron and tore at her blouse, pushing her to the bed in the corner. "First, this," he panted, "the thing you owe me." With her apron strings, he tied her hands and fell on her. "If you scream, I'll cut your throat," he warned and then whispered in her ear, "It's for this I came. . . The recipes are for her and mother, only my tickets to you." He bore down on her, raping and ravishing, one hand over her mouth. Finished, he lay on her exhausted. Seconds later, taking a deeper breath, he repeated the act, pinning her down and kissing her mouth. For a moment, all was still. Mara let her tears slide, as Oleg stroked and groped all over her body and then spoke in her ear. "Now, be a good girl and give me the recipe. Where is it?"

"Up in the tree," she said, suddenly rising, trying to break the strings that bound her.

Oleg slapped her face. "How dare you make fun of me?"

"I'm not. It really is up in a tree," she said, laughing hysterically.

"Stop it! Stop laughing when nothing is funny," Oleg said and held her down, watching her laughter turn into cries and moans. "We won't give up, and you know it, my dear *Hexe,* so stop lying!" For a second, he smiled, looking down on her. "It was good, yes? You liked it, and we can do it again, but now get up!" he ordered and untied her hands but held them fast. "Go and get it!" With one hand, he pulled out a drawer and dug through it. He saw some papers written all over with words in columns that looked like recipes and dug deeper.

"Give me what I'm asking, or I'll have to kill you!"

"Yes, I believe you would and you may," Mara gave in, trembling, trying to pull herself upright and looking for a way out, but Olga stood in the doorway with Oleg's dagger in her hand.

"You will never find the recipe, because it is not written down," Mara said, taking a deep breath, looking out at the hovering hills, from where would come her help." Calmly, she turned her eyes to meet Oleg's. "You see, my life's mysterious and precious recipe hides in my heart and hands and—in my soul."

"Don't joke and play games with me!" shouted Oleg, his scar glowing. "I'm not joking, and I'd never play games with you!"

"Oho! Then I'll have to cut it out of your heart and hands and soul, piece by piece."

"Do it!" hissed Olga. "Be a man! Here's your dagger."

"Yes, be a man!" said Mara. "So you will kill me. Throw me in the oven and then burn down my house and disappear. Like they did," she added, still trembling, staring at him, and saw that he was as afraid as a cornered tiger pup, glancing around, not knowing which way to go, what to do. She pulled her torn clothes about her and faced him. "I know how the story will go. The news will spread that another *Bakkerhexe* has lured poor, innocent children into this *Hexenwald* to eat them, but that angels came down from heaven and saved them by burning down her devil-enchanted house. Yes, they will come to look at the place, find the ovens, the ruins, but no sign of the *Hexe*. By then, you and your sister will be in Fernau, baking away, becoming richer and richer until you will choke on your own greed. Oh, yes, my friend, I know the story. I now know what happened to Katharina. Your parents must have told you all about it—the trial and all. I see that you're following the story, step by step, don't you?" She edged backward into the kitchen, keeping her eyes on Oleg, trying to get a hold of her iron skillet but could not before he pinned back her arms.

"Yes, and we'll start another hunt and you'll burn. If I can't have you, no one will!" he growled, staring at her face and then her hands. "They're large, like shovels, but soft," he said and clasped his face between them. "Heal that scar! Hold me! Be mine!"

"No!" She tried to say it calmly, reasonably, trying to free herself.

"Kiss the scar you made—— with your magic lips ... Hold me with your magic hands." He now pleaded like a child, with tears in his eyes. She let her fingers trace the scar.

"Kiss it!"

"No! Please go away!" She also spoke in a gentle, pleading tone.

"I want to lie with you and sleep," he said, fondling her, dragging her back to the bed. She screamed and broke loose.

"Don't touch me! Go away before it's too late," she warned. She was ready to tell him that the dwarfs would be bursting into the room any minute and that blood would be flowing, but he was twisting her arm again. "Go! Take your sister and run!" she cried out, suddenly taking pity on the miserable, misguided overgrown children.

"First, the damned recipe! Give it to me!"

"Let go, and I'll write something down."

"Really? You will?"

"A promise is a promise."

"*Hexe! Bakkerhexe!*" Oleg shouted, excited, squeezing her hard against him.

"You're sick!" Mara scolded. "No recipe is worth spilling blood, you fools! Let go, and I'll write what you want, do what you want. Just go, go away! Run, both of you!"

"Trying to scare us, huh?" Quickly Olga threw a rope around her from behind, but Oleg shouted for her to get out, to keep watch and not come back until he called. "I'm not finished with her!"

Olga stepped out. Facing each other inside the sunlit kitchen, Oleg held Mara close, again taking her hands, stroking his face with them. "You said you'd give me what I want. You know what I want, don't you?" He picked her up and carried her to the bed and laid her down again.

She kicked and cried, saying, "They'll be here. They'll kill you! Go away!" "I'll never leave you! We'll take you with us, and you can bake for us again. I've wanted you ever since you branded me. I carry you always in my

face, and your heart belongs to me!" "No!"

"Yes!" He took his hands off her. "Why don't you run away? Isn't it good with us? You liked it, didn't you? You've thought about me all this time. You wished me here, so you'd be rid of that milksop." He pulled her face up to his. "Kiss the scar so it heals," he said, pushing his cheek against her lips. She bit him, cutting the skin. Enraged, he forced his way inside her again. "Now we're even at last," he said and repeated the act with more force, more insatiable, savage pleasure.

"Now let's kill her and throw her into one of her ovens," Olga cheered, jumping around, all excited because she had seen it all. "Let's see if she'll burn. If she burns, she's a witch, and if she don't, she is also a witch. So we win both ways. You stab her and we'll drag her out. I know which oven is the hottest."

"The recipe!" Mara screamed. "I must write it down." "Quickly! Do it!" Olga shouted.

"I need paper and my quill!" Mara cried out, trying to pull herself together, to cover herself.

Oleg threw a sheet around her and, holding her hand fast, led her to her desk and watched as, with trembling hands, she wrote a list of ingredients. She paused and tried to think how to write down the directions, thinking that her saviors should be very close by now. "I cannot, cannot write it down so you'll understand. It's easy. Just mix the things, knead, and bake, but now get lost, both of you!"

"She's trying to fool us again," Olga shouted and gagged her. Then they tied her hands and feet.

That's how it was, Mara thought and went limp in Oleg's hard grip, cleansed from fear, thinking about Katharina. Oleg pulled the ropes tighter.

"Don't be scared. We'll keep you tied down until we get our horses and wagon. We'll take you home, away from here, back where you belong."

"No, let's burn her," Olga cried out excitedly, pricking Mara's feet with needles until they bled. "How many times do you have to prick your buns to let the air out?" Olga's hands pinched Mara's cheeks, untied the rag over her mouth, and, bearing down on her, pinched her lips. "Tell me, pretty please, for now I am the *Bakkerhexe.*"

"Leave her alone!" Oleg yelled. "She belongs to me."

Suddenly, Olga screamed. Blood gushed from her leg. She let go of her victim and saw that the room was full of small black-bearded men. They jumped on Oleg, thrusting their daggers into him and pushing Olga against the hot oven door.

"Kill her! She's the devil!" shouted a little woman. "I saw what they did to her."

"Don't kill!" Mara called. "Let them go! Take my recipes, all of them! Oleg, get up and run!"

But her words came too late. Daggers pierced both twins' lungs and hearts. With a howl, Olga fell over her brother. Quickly, the women cut the ropes that tied Mara and carried her to the spring. They washed off the blood and cleaned her wounds with its pure and icy water and dried her with clean towels.

"It's over at last." Mara heaved and rocked herself, watching red water ripple over the rocks and dissolve. "It's finished, done and finished," she spoke in a trance, rocking and crying. "I know now the truth. I know how women were turned into witches and burned. It's they—the greedy and mighty—who light the pyres. And for what?

"So that is how she died. Now I know." Mara wept, leaning over the bank and washing her face and eyes. She stared into the water, frightened by her distorted, rippling image that multiplied inside the waves. "There they are— the *raganas, witches, Hexen,* rising out of the waters. Now I know that their spirits roam the earth," she spoke dazed, "finding no rest, no justice, becoming subjects for stories and paintings, where they live forever like evil ghosts—ugly and gnarled, scaring children, while the devils dance and clap their hands. Oh, heaven, send down your rains and wash our sins away! Pluck out the roots of lust and greed like thorns and thistles! Oh, Mother of God, save me!" As though seeking the face of angels, she stepped back from the water's edge and, lying back, searched the clouds.

When she rose up, she saw the dwarfs, shovels swung over their shoulders, disappear into the woods. She saw others carrying the wrapped-up bleeding bodies of Olga and Oleg. She cried out, ready to run after them, but the women held her back, asking her to tell them her true story. Quietly, calmly, she did, but the little women understood nothing, because she spoke and cried in her own old Livonian language.

When the dwarf men, after the burial, crossed the spring, she brushed away her tears and stood up. She watched them walk away as if they had chopped up nothing more than some dead branches. They started singing some strange hymn of victory, as if they were marching home from war. She shivered, wrapping her arms around herself, while the sun burned her with its noonday rays. Shielding her eyes, she stared at her cottage and thought about Heinrich.

"I'll never go inside it again," she said and asked the women to go and fetch her traveling clothes and pack more clothes and some food into her carpetbag. She told them where her money was hidden. "Bring it all out. I'll divide it evenly between us. There will be enough for your wages and my way home. Yes, it is time for me to go home, back to my country, back to where I came from."

While she waited, she started picking flowers, pulling the daisies and bluebells by their roots, and making garlands. Three. She stumbled to Katharina's grave, to the oven Heinrich never repaired, and hung one wreath on the crude wooden cross he had put up and crossed herself. "You were so silly," she said. "You could have saved us all. You could have given Hans Metzler what he wanted. Why were *you* so greedy? And why did you choose me?"

She stumbled on until she came upon the fresh mound. She broke branches and covered the raw, turned-up earth and put both wreaths over them. She crossed herself twice and leaned against the aspen tree, looking up, watching the bright blue sky through the small trembling leaves, feeling her tears flood her eyes and rain down her face. She wept for all the aborted lives, all with hands and mouths and feet—working, striving to be and become, to make a difference in life. She imagined souls that bargained with God or the devil for the wealth of this world. *We are all the offspring of Cain, all conceived and born in sin, so the church teaches, but do I believe it? Am I closer to the truth now after all this wandering and laboring and suffering? No, I'm still a little girl lost in the woods ...*

Strange currents went through her body as she felt Oleg's crime mix with hers and her guilt, recalling their connection from beginning to end; she thought about her mother and the baron, her father, and her mother's lawful husband, who never tasted her love ... Again, she felt Oleg's first lust-laden look, followed by his groin hard up against her, and a shiver like a flame burned her insides, making her double up in heaves. After she raised her head and looked at the sky and the tall tree hiding the recipe, she took the locket with the large *R* off her neck. She opened it and put Roland's lock of hair to her lips, whispering, "Forgive me, but I must break my promise. I have taken part in murder. My lips could never kiss yours again." She fell on her knees and, with one hand, scraped a hole in the soft earth and lined it with grass. She kissed the locket and laid it to rest and covered it with daisy blossoms, mumbling, "*He loves me, loves me not . . .*" Then she pulled the earth over the tiny mound, like a blemish. *So many lives ... cut up and for what? Why?*

She stood up, looking down, her tears flowing, her mind in a daze. After what seemed a lifetime, she waded back through the brush and tall grass, back to her house, where the women were quietly waiting, her bag packed. She asked them to go bring her paper and quill and wrote a note to Heinrich:

My friend, I am grateful for all you have done for me, but I cannot live here anymore. I cannot look at you after what was done to me. I am no longer what I was. If you want to know more, ask our friends, who saved my life. With all my heart, I wish you good fortune and God's blessing. So, farewell, my faithful knight! Forgive me, please. —Be happy and live! Mara.

After a last look at her house that had sheltered her for over a year, she stumbled up the mountain path. On top, she turned and looked back on the valley, so green, so lovely, so innocent. She saw the white birds flying, picking up crumbs from around her yard, and flying back to the lake to feed their young.

A sharp whistle startled her. She turned and saw two dwarfs, armed with axes, come toward her. They offered to show her the shortest path through the woods to the highway. She said she was going north. They nodded and ran ahead and back around her, warning and admonishing her to hide whenever they met anyone.

By evening, they had guided her out onto the open highway and pointed to a booth on the right side, with signs pointing to the cities in the north. Exhausted and hurting, she thanked them and watched them vanish back into the woods. For a while, she stood waiting for the coach, but realizing that none would come this late, she went inside the booth. She curled up in a corner, pulled her cloak over her, and fell asleep.

The next morning, after a restless night of disconnected thoughts and dreams, all tangled with pain, shame, and fears, she viewed the road. In her haphazard sleeping and waking, she imagined returning to the Castle of Wenden, her father welcoming her, perhaps Roland riding up the path to take her in his arms, the skylarks singing and flowers blooming all around the castle walls. But then she imagined the questions, the stories about old *raganas* and then telling her own story. At that, her heart stood still. She sat up, wide awake. "No!" she exclaimed. "I cannot go back."

The lies … she would have to garnish her story with lies, for the truth was too awful. She did not even know what the truth was—who was innocent and who guilty, and how evil gave way to goodness and goodness to evil. No, she could not answer the many questions that had no answers, and she knew that the old castle with its crimes and ghosts could never again be her happy home. She relived her flight from Wenden and the trauma and abuses that caused her to escape. A current of fear sent another shiver through her. As descending from the night clouds, to her mind, came the images of *Frau* Liebman and her daughters, Angelina and Sophia—all who had worked together to be rid of her. Mara stared at the darkness, thinking, *Time has passed. No doubt my stepsisters are profitably married. Perhaps by now they are respected baronesses of their own castles or manors. They have claimed all their inherent rights and have power of their own, and if I suddenly appeared, there would be trouble, even another witch hunt, no doubt urged by Stepmother. The Herr, my father, would be helpless as usual, perhaps hiding in his tower, recalling and reveling in the passions of his youth. And Roland? He likewise would be out of my reach, out of the sound of my voice. If I would tell him the truth, he would flee from me because he loved me while I was an innocent victim—chaste and pure. But a damaged one he could never accept and heal with his love. He would not understand, and he, too, would escape into his lordly rights and marry a princess chosen for him. No, there is no way back. There, I would not be welcome even as a baker.*

She stood up and clutched herself around her waist. *No! I will never bake for those who hurt my people! Never will I slave for selfish lords and heartless executioners!*

She leaned against a post. Nearly swooning, she slid back onto the bench, holding her head as if shielding herself from the image of the *Henker,* who appeared to her troubled mind as a grotesque, apelike monster gloating overhead, with cookie crumbs in his beard, smelling of ginger and blood. The thought of ginger alone made her nauseous.

Trembling, suddenly wide awake, she lifted herself up and, gathering all her strength, staggered across the highway, determined to board the first coach going south, down toward Nürnberg. She would find the Abbey in Quedlinburg, where Katharina Schraderin had baked, and seek shelter and peace there. Perhaps, in time, she would write her true story and fight for justice that would eliminate such evils that cause witch hunts, wars, and persecutions of innocent people. *Perhaps* ... she braced herself ... *perhaps there is a new and innocent life inside me? What shall we do, then?* She did not know. She did not know whether to despair or to hope. The sun had not yet risen, and thick fog tangled all around her.

Waiting and shivering, she stared at her hands. They were rough, chapped, and cold. They were tired and empty hands, hands that he, the victimizer and victim, had held and that had touched the scar on his cheek, hands that had fed the monstrous executioner and a band of others who had ruled over her life and soul. Such guilty hands could never embrace those who loved her. They needed redemption. And those hands, she swore, would never bake again. Not for profit. Only for her daily bread and bread for those who were truly hungry and poor.

She clasped her hands as in prayer, pleading her case, asking forgiveness. As she glanced around, afraid of being pursued and questioned, to her troubled mind, like a balm, came the words of the Old One: *Human hands need to touch divine hands. They need to connect, to feel the flow of blood and power and celestial energy first before they can do something rare and wonderful.*

Chilled by a whiff of the north wind, she raised her hands to heaven and reached, reached for the morning star paling on the horizon. And then she heard the waking birdcalls and the drumming of horses' hoofs. The stagecoach was fast approaching, rolling out of the fleeting darkness toward her, to take her into a new day and a new world.

THE END

Epilogue

The year is 1812. Mara's great-great-granddaughter is nearly eighty. Her gait is strong, her sight still sharp. She lives in Bavaria, in the foothills of the Alps in a charming little Tyrolean-style house displaying a mural of the parable about the Good Shepherd and his lost sheep. She is the mother of six children, grand- and great-great-grandmother of over a dozen. Everyone calls her Oma, and her white-hair, white-bearded husband Opa. It is the time of Advent, with snow covering the higher mountain slopes, while the pastures are still green, with grazing sheep like a Christmas card. Oma and Opa have taken the slow train to Garmisch, where they plan to buy presents for their younger grand- and great-grandchildren at the *Weinachtsmarkt.*

Like children themselves, the two old people, gleefully, with cups of *Rotwein* warming their hands, mill around the marketplace. At one booth, they see a mock gingerbread house and a gnarled-faced, crooked-nosed witch selling cookies. Girls in *dirndl dresses* and boys in *lederhosen* are behind the counter helping her. To scare or entertain the crowd of children pressing around the booth, at times, the witch scolds and threatens to throw them into the oven—if they don't work hard enough and don't obey their parents. At the end of each spontaneous skit, she spreads her arms over the crowd, pushes her hideous masked face forward, and issues mean growling noises, ending with a high-pitched laugh. The children act scared and scamper away, while a new bunch takes their place.

Oma and Opa buy boxes of candies colorfully wrapped to be hung on their Christmas tree. Oma stops at the cookie booth, but Opa pulls her away, saying that she can bake much better than anything he sees. She smiles, and they move on to the next stop, where happy elves in bright costumes sell pretty handmade toys. Behind the counter, they see a stage with a painted backdrop of woods and caves. There, the elves do acrobatics, dance, and sing, playing ancient lutes, drums, and horns. At certain times, they perform a short version of a new play: *Snow White and the Seven Dwarfs.*

The couple watches the skit; they buy various toys and go on until they come to a book stand. Impatiently, Opa shuffles about, holding a full net bag, while Oma's right hand carefully, hardly touching the covers, glides over beautifully illustrated children's books. It stops on *Hausmärchen der Brüder Grimm.* The vendor assures her that this is the latest book by the young Brothers Grimm, who will surely win every child's heart the world over. "It's the rage," he says, "sure to be a bestseller that would last for ages to come," and then turns away, calling, "Yes, yes, come one, come all!" Oma buys several copies for her grand- and great-grandchildren and one for herself. Opa scowls but unties his coin pouch and pays up and then lifts his full knapsack, swings it over his shoulder, and, with Oma carrying the net bag and keeping in step, they hurry to the train station. The short day is darkening quickly.

The following week until Christmas Eve, Oma mixes, rolls, cuts, and bakes *Lebkuchen* and other cookies, while Opa hangs ornaments and clips candles on the big fir tree he had brought down from higher grounds. Oma wraps the Brothers Grimm books and loses herself in deep thoughts, pondering, wondering, and remembering stories about witches and goblins and how the uncles and grandfathers enjoyed scaring children and, when satisfied, smoked their pipes and laughed like naughty elves. But Oma, when little, was not scared. She was curious, for she was hearing regularly unclear bits and pieces of stories about witches who had lived long ago deep in the near and far mountain ranges, hiding in thickets and caves. She remembers the aunts telling tales about witch hunts and burnings and how many women throughout the old kingdoms were caught, thrown in dungeons, and burned alive. She remembers that she had cried in pity for the poor witches and that the grown-ups would never answer her why such things were done.

As she was growing older and wiser and kept hearing her mother and grandmother still talking in hushed tones about old times and unjust laws, her curiosity never ceased. Years later, she set out to find out the truth. She visited the closest convents of the district but, in the end, found nothing concrete. No times and places, no names. As if with one voice, the superior nuns answered that, yes, there were witch hunts all over the Holy Roman Empire and that many women were captured, even burned, and—naturally— many sought refuge in the convents. One superior volunteered her observations, saying that the refugees were usually talented women who had gotten in trouble: some pregnant, others running away from abusive men; yet others were adult orphans with no homes of their own, but most of them were smart and very talented in many arts—cooking, baking, stitching tapestries, and painting on canvases that decorated many dark halls. But even she could not or did not dare give out any names, saying that more women called themselves Mary or Maria than she could count.

Disappointed, Oma soon gave up her search for the truth. Also, by then, the time had come for her to marry and set up her own household, and it was not long before she had enough children to keep her busy. She turned her eyes to the future, leaving the befuddled past behind.

On this Christmas Eve, in the afternoon, she rested while the last batch of her *Lebkuchen* cooled. After she woke up from her nap and finished frosting them, she sat down in her rocking chair by the fireplace and opened her new book. She leafed through it, looking at the illustrations, and came upon *Hänsel und Gretel und die Knusperhexe.*

Without warning, of its own accord, her heart, strangely excited, starts to jump. She reads the story carefully and studies the illustrations. The first shows a beautifully detailed path into the woods, with little Hansel and Gretel holding hands and going as if into the sunset. On the next pages, she sees drawings of the poor lost children, the gingerbread house, and the witch, leaning on a cane, a black cat at the hem of her skirt. The witch is bending over, peering into the cage, and testing Hansel's finger. And there is Gretel, composed and clever, pushing the witch into a huge oven. *Ach so! The Grimm Brothers have stamped those smart, young women as old and evil, turning them into cannibals, kidnappers, thieves, and sorcerers who are so dangerous that even the smallest child will learn that it is a good thing to push them into ovens like loaves of brown bread!*

Oma, afraid that her heart might give out, puts the book aside and goes to mix some drops of her own concoction in a glass of spring water and drinks it slowly, standing at the window, watching soft, large snowflakes float and whirl as they cover the earth. She returns to her rocking chair and studies the illustrations, thinking that she had seen them before—the country road, the woods with huts hidden under large trees, and elves dancing in a meadow.

But where? she wonders, watching the logs shoot out orange and purple flames. *Ach ja!* —Suddenly, the illustration of the road into the woods, except for the children, reminds her of the tapestry that hung on her grandmother's wall, behind her large bed. *It was such a long time ago* ... However, in that tapestry, instead of the children, a man and a woman wrapped in a gray floating cape were galloping down the path on a black horse. When she had asked her mother to tell the story again, her grandmother had told her that the young woman was her own great-grandmother Maria, whom her knight was rescuing from a dungeon where she had been thrown because people said that she was a witch because she could bake magic cookies ... As Oma, when little, pestered *her* Oma, wanting to know more, she got a scolding with "You're too little to understand."

"*Yes, don't ask. You're too little* ..." Oma heard those phrases often, but that never stopped her curiosity. Now, she wants to know what really happened. Who was the woman on the horse? Why and where was the horse made to gallop like the wind, his hoofs stitched high off the ground?

Oma wipes her glasses and, turning the pages, peers into every illustration. And slowly to her mind comes another tapestry she had seen on another wall, showing a cookie house behind a large tree, next to a running brook, where elves dance in a round. She also remembers a set of tea towels with wild weeping willows over a grave and a faded apron with "*Bakkerhexe*" stitched in red on a white bodice. One of her aunts used to wear that apron. *What happened to it?* She vaguely recalls the aunt telling her that it and other fine needlework was done by *her* great- or great-great-grandmother in a convent. Her name was Maria, but she was not German. The aunt did not know who she was and where she had come from.

So, was my great-great-grandmother Maria stitching her life story? Did she ever finish it, and how did it end? And who am I? Where do I come from?

She stops posing these and more questions. She vaguely remembers a large tapestry on an abbey wall in Quedlinburg, in which was stitched a very similar scene as that in the new book she was holding: a rider racing through the woods; a scene with gingerbread houses, and two bleeding dogs. *Could all this be related? Could it be a part of my history?* she wonders, as her hands burrow deeper inside the book until Opa walks through the door, telling her that he has finished decorating the fir tree and snatches a cookie. "Ah! Mmm … It's the best! The real thing. Must be in your hands, *mein Liebchen,* this art of baking."

"Yes … Perhaps," Oma says, aroused from her trance. Smiling sadly, she gives him the largest *Lebkuchen* and wishes him a joyful Christmas.

That's all.

Author's Notes

Reference and source: Hans Traxler, *Die Wahrheit über Hänsel und Gretel,* with photographs by Peter V. Tresckow, *Rowohlt Taschenbuch Verlag GmbH*, Reinbeck at Hamburg, March 1983.

This 115-page paperback tells a most fascinating story about the research of a Czechoslovakian teacher Georg Ossegg, born May 21, 1919, in Prague, who had developed a keen interest in finding the background sources of the stories by the brothers Jacob and Wilhelm Grimm. Among others, Ossegg discovered that behind *Hänsel and Gretel and the Witch* were real people and the real witch trial (1647) of Katharina Schraderin (b. 1618), who, until 1638, worked in the Abbey of Quedlinburg and sold her cookies at the local market. Hans Metzler, the court baker of Nürenberg, spotted her and wanted her *Lebkuchen* recipe, which she would not give him. He accused her of being a witch and turned her in for a trial. She defended herself well and was found not guilty. However, Metzler still pursued her as she fled north, settling in the woods of Engelsberg, where, almost two hundred years later, the Brothers Grimm found source materials for their stories. That region became known as *Hexenwald* (witches' woods) and for a long time was believed to be haunted. There, Katharina mysteriously disappeared, and there, Georg Ossegg of Prague conducted an archeological dig and found in a buried oven the bones of Katharina and her baking materials. Hans and his sister, Greta, who served as her brother's witness, then thirty-seven and thirty-four, respectively, were never found out as the alleged murderers of the innocent, successful baker, known as the *Bakkerhexe*—baker-witch. Instead, brother and sister, in the German endearing diminutives as *Hänsel* and *Gretchen,* have gone into history and every culture as the poor innocent children who were nearly eaten up by a cannibalistic, wicked witch.

Traxler writes, "Based on Georg Ossegg's research results, especially after the excavations in Spessart, there is no longer any doubt that ... the brothers knew the whole truth about Hänsel and Gretel but for ethical reasons prudently concealed it" (p. 17). However, Traxler could not establish what and *how much* the Grimm brothers knew about the trial and outcome of Katharina Schraderin and why, in creating the Hänsel and Gretel story, they turned the innocent baker into a hideous witch. Traxler also emphasizes the fact that this was a well-known witch hunt and trial case, and people talked about it far and wide for many years. He cites a letter from Jacob to Wilhelm Grimm, where he writes that the real story would be useful for their collection but that it would work better if the witch were ... well, the way she is in the folk tale read all over the world (p. 90). It is clear that the brothers took Metzler's fantastic accusations of Katharina Schraderin at her trial and created the well-known, much-loved story on which, in turn, Engelbart Humperdinck, in 1893, based his successful, ever-popular opera.

I have translated and included the biographical facts and trial of Schraderin as set down in Traxler's book, pages 73–79, and included the translation of the court proceedings of the witch hunt and the trial in *The Coveted Recipe*.

After I read *Die Wahrheit über Hänsel und Gretel*, I was deeply moved by the tragedy behind the story I have known since my childhood in three languages—Latvian, German, and English. With my children, I had made gingerbread houses, baked *Lebkuchen* and *Pfefferkuchen*, taken the children to the opera, and bought different versions of the fairy tale. But once *The Truth about Hänsel and Gretel* came into my hands, the story and the opera, traditionally performed at Christmas time, lost its appeal.

I—a World War II child refugee from Latvia—felt an urge to write another story where I, too, try to penetrate the truth and guess what might have happened long ago—once upon a time, in the Dark Ages or where darkness, prejudice, greed, superstition, and other deadly sins rule over innocent human lives. As I studied history and literature and looked down through the ages, I saw that history repeats itself in many variations, and human nature—with its good, evil, and mixed characteristics—does not change but goes on even in our modern age. In that spirit, I began writing *The Coveted Recipe*.

The idea for the novel came to me in Berlin in the spring of 1991, two years after the fall of the Berlin Wall. A teacher who had lived behind the Wall in East Berlin took me on an excursion to the nearby charming medieval town Bernau, still inside the old city wall, with a moat all around. Close to the gate still stands an imposing two-story brick house through which runs the old wall. That house was the residence of the executioner (*Henker*) and is now a museum. The description of this strange house, the tower, torture equipment, etc., are exactly as described in my story.

When, about five years after my visit to Bernau, I received and read Hans Traxler's book *Die Wahrheit über Hänsel und Gretel,* everything came into focus. With all that I had met and the specific knowledge about Katharina Schraderin—the baker falsely accused as a witch and brutally murdered— gave substance to a gothic novel, featuring the ill-conceived but beautiful and extraordinarily talented Mara, I began writing. I named my heroine Mara, because the name in Latvian folklore is that of the earth goddess but in the biblical context means "*bitter.*" Thus, the name is symbolically rich, as befitting multitudes of past and present victims whose lives were and are affected by forces beyond them and their control. As Mara, so many suffer for the sins of their fathers and mothers, which multiply and affect new cycles of lives as time flows on.

Ragana in the Latvian language is the word for "witch," but it does not quite have the same connotations as in American English, with its commonly known Halloween images. *Ragana* is an ancient word whose basic meaning deals with *seeing, foreseeing, knowledge, wisdom, cunning, cleverness.* The attributes of evil came with Christianization of the Baltic area and the Catholic Church's struggle with paganism. Then *raganas* became associated with the devil and other evils. Thus, the earlier *raganas* in Latvia had been and still are depicted as unusual and intelligent old women, as well as young, beautiful, and chaste virgins. They were honored and respected as prophets, healers, and advisors. As such, they were manipulated by powerful men and envied by jealous women. Generally, in primitive agrarian society, when brought to trial, *raganas* were accused of outlandish acts, such as bewitching men sexually and immorally. They were also blamed for inexplicable phenomena of nature, such as crop failures and blights, livestock sickness and deaths—all punishable by torturous death, such as burning at the stake. Because the present image of the gnarled, old ugly witch only partially fit the raganas of Livonia, I have also used the Latvian word in the story.

The most active period of witch hunts in Livonia happened during the seventeenth to mid-eighteenth centuries. There are recorded burnings of woods and smoking out of caves where the *raganas* hid. Luckily, the witch hunts and burnings at stake never reached the height they had during the Inquisition in other countries of Europe, where approximately one hundred thousand innocent women lost their lives.

Excerpt from *The Silver Veil*

I became more than casually interested in the *ragana* (witch) theme after translating two poetry dramas by the eminent Latvian writer Aspazija (pseudonym for Elza Rozenberga, 1965–1943). The protagonists are strong, intelligent, beautiful women, such as Liesma, "flame," in *Ragana* (1895) and Guna, "fire," in *Sidraba šķidrauts (The Silver Veil,* 1905; translation 1975.) Both dramas are symbolic, where national ambitions and women's rights— then highly censored—are camouflaged. In the opening scene, Guna, *a woman of the new age,* defines herself to a superstitious crowd:

How can I help you?
I am neither a sorceress nor a prophetess.
I do not go about at midnight
In search of magic herbs to cure your ills.
I conjure neither good nor evil spirits.
My strength is my own spirit!
And if it sees more clearly and perceives more deeply
Than your spirit, then be aware of this:
Each human spirit which does probe into the past And then into the future
Is like a legendary god with many eyes
And is indeed a fortune-teller and a prophet
Who sees what is behind and what is yet to come.
When in the change of times
The centuries crack and rift asunder,
Then, like an eagle, the human spirit flies above the dark abyss
And lands on higher summits of the future.

If my voice does echo deep within your hearts
And if it wakens and excites you, it merely puts into words
That which unexpressed and dormant lies within you.
My goddess gave to me this silver veil, which puts me in a different state:
These tiny, fragile silver threads like living nerves guide all my senses.
I see a three-fold vision: I feel, I hear
The silent tremor of each leaf,
And likewise do I feel your pain.
I sing a lullaby to all mankind,
That plaintive melody of deepest longing That beats upon the human ear
Like distant ocean waves from timeless seas—
Those waves have tossed us all upon life's jagged rocks
Where roses of our dreams cannot take root.
This subterranean melody flows with us everywhere
Like secret longing for our own annihilation
Mingled with eternal thirst for life.
It rings and rings
And calls us back from whence we came.

The Silver Veil, Act I, sc.iv

Important dates:

1480 – The Church denounced all activity and incentives that took place outside the church's supervision and without its blessing. *Raganas/ragani* were proclaimed as having connections with the devil and evil spirits; therefore, those people who were viewed as such were regarded as dangerous —evil possessed; good people would not associate with them, and those who did would naturally be suspect. The Church made this view official, stating that

1. *Raganas* (plural, feminine) and *ragani* (plural, masculine) have signe oath with the devil and lead immoral lives.
2. They reject the Christian faith and the teachings of the Church collaborate with evil forces.
3. With the help of evil forces they harm people and destroy property.
4. They fly through the air and can turn into various animals. They also can people into animals and inanimate objects.

Because of such a decree, suspicion could be generated against any unusual individual. Common belief developed that *raganas* met and performed their acts in secret, as in the dark hours of the night, and in great hurry before sunrise. They would hide from people and live in caves and woods. Especially dangerous and quick would be their activities on midsummer night, when they could bewitch the cattle and bring harm to crops, etc. Therefore, bundles of nettles, red clover, and other magic grasses would be tied to gate posts as antidotes.

*A solitary figure stands in the middle of a fire. Whether
the Hero is self-immolating from the ardor of a burning,
sacred flame of inner conviction, or is enduring a scorching
conflagration set by exterior forces of attempted censorship
and/or de-humanization − the Hero must needs submit to the
ordeal of Trial by Fire.*
(Sculpture: S. Janson-Ruņģis, Altars and Myths, "A Hero's
Journey.")

The last recorded burning in Livonia was in **1692** and the beheading in **1699**. The persecutions in Livonia came to an end after certain women were accused for bewitching an estate owner's cows that stopped giving milk. At that trial in Riga (circa **1646–50),** an accused woman defended herself by stating that everybody has some ability to do something unusual and that if the court wants to burn everybody, then there will be no one to work in the fields. However, that did not mean that, suddenly, superstition was eradicated. The prejudice against unusually beautiful and clever, or wise, age- bent women continued well beyond that time.[4]

1618 – Katharina Schraderin, born as the seventh child of a coalminer of Wernigerode.

1634 – Age sixteen, placed in the Abbey of Quedlinburg, where she worked in the kitchen until **1638.** During this time, she became famous for her ***Lebkuchen*** and other fine pastries, which she sold locally and then moved on to the Nürnberg market. "There the royal court baker confronted her about the already world-famous Lebkuchen, which would mean a fine income. His name was **Hans Metzler**" (Traxler, 73).

1647 – Beginning with Katherina's escape in the night with her baking equipment. She found an abandoned small house, had it remodeled, and built four ovens outside and resumed her business.
High point of witch hunts in this part of Germany.

1648 – Hans Metzler continues his life in Nürnberg and is in good standing. Dies in **1660.**

1812 – First publication of **Jacob Ludwig Carl** (1785–1863) and **Wilhelm Carl** (1786–1859) **Grimms** *Kinder- und Hausmärchen,* "a work which formed a foundation for the science of comparative folklore" (*Chambers Biographical Dictionary,* Edinburgh, 1894).

1893 – **Engelbart Humperdinck** (1854–1921) with librettist **Adel Heid Wette** creates the opera *Hänsel und Gretel.*

1945 – **Georg Ossegg,** a teacher, arrives in Spessart with his students who were evacuated from Prague after World War II.

1962 – **Ossegg** begins his archeological digs and research about the background of The Brothers Grimm story of *Hänsel and Gretel.*

1983 – **Hans Traxler's** book *Die Wahrheit über Hänsel und Gretel* (The truth about Hansel and Gretel, the documentary of the fairy tale by Brothers Grimm with photographs by **Peter V. Tresckow**) is published by Rowohlt Press.[5]

Appendix

GERMAN LEBKUCHEN

Honey mixture: 2 lb honey, 2 T butter, 6 T water
1 lb sugar
pour hot over flour mixture
3 lb flour (10–12 cups)
½ T citron, chopped fine,
cardamom, pinch ginger
2 T ground cloves
grated peel of 1 orange and 1 lemon
Cinnamon, 1 t salt

After pouring hot honey mix over flour mix, add 2 t hartshorn dissolved in a little water.

Let cool. Then add 8 egg yolks + 2 t potash (potassium bicarbonate), dissolved in a little water. Let stand at room temp for about 8 days. Roll out 1/4" thick, cut into forms, and bake very slowly. Cover with white chocolate frosting. (Can be also in flat loaf and decorated with almonds and then cut in squares while hot.)

———

Heritage of Cooking: A Collection of Recipes from East Perry County, Missouri, 1895, Friedenberg, MO, founded 1844, "The Hill of Peace."

LATVIAN PIPARKŪKAS

⅓ cup honey
½ cup molasses or sorghum
1 cup dark brown sugar
½ lb butter
3 tablespoons pork lard
2½ cups unbleached white flour

<u>Prepare, combine, and set aside:</u> 1 teaspoon ground ginger
1 teaspoon cinnamon
½ teaspoon pepper
½ teaspoon ground cloves
1 teaspoon ground nutmeg, cardamom, coriander
2 beaten eggs
2¼ cups unbleached white flour (maybe half white, half whole wheat)
¼ teaspoon baking soda
1 egg for basting; optional: chopped almonds for garnish Directions:

1. Combine first five ingredients in a medium-size saucepan and mix them rigorously to a bubbling boil.
2. Remove from heat and add all at once the 2½ cups of flour and spices.
3. Blend and mix thoroughly until the batter bubbles. Then set aside to cool; gently turn over a couple of times to even the temperature.
4. After the dough has cooled down to lukewarm, add the two beaten eggs and mix them into the dough; then add the second portion of flour, a handful at a time (more or less as needed), until comfortable for thorough kneading. When the dough turns glossy and does not stick to your hands, form it into a ball and put it into a lightly buttered bowl, cover it with wax paper and tea towel and let it rest, even as you, too, take a deserved rest.

When the dough is cool and can be easily handled, roll it out (a handful at a time) as thinly as possible and cut it into desirable forms. Or you may keep it refrigerated for an indefinite time until you will be in the mood to bake.

Preheat the oven at 350 °F. Baking time is about 10 minutes, but watch carefully and remove quickly from pans when golden brown.

Suggestion: line the cookie sheets with parchment paper to protect from burning.

Other books by Astrida B. Stahnke

Stahnke, *Astrida B. Aspazija: Her Life and Her Drama*. Lanham, New York, London: University Press of America, 1984. Includes biographical sketch of Aspazija and English translations of her verse dramas *The Silver Veil* (Sidraba šķidrauts, 1905) and *The Serpent's Bride* (*Zalša līgava*, 1928).

—. *Aspazija: Ragana/The Silver Veil*. Riga: Pils, 2003. Includes an introduction and English translations of Aspazija's verse dramas *The Silver Veil* and *Ragana* (*The Witch*, 1895).

—. *Aspazija: A Latvian Writer 1865–1943. Her Lyrical Prose*. Jūrmala: The Literature and Music Museum of Latvia, 2015. Includes excerpts in English translations from Aspazija's autobiography, short stories, fantasies, a novella from Aspazija: *Kopoti Raksti* (collected works):6. Riga: Liesma, 1988.

—. *The Golden Steed. Translation of Zelta Zirgs* by Rainis, 1909, in *The Golden Steed: Seven Baltic Plays*, ed. Alfreds Straumanis. Prospect Heights, Illinois: Waveland Press, 1979.

—. *How Long Is Exile?* Novel in three parts. Book 1: The Song and Dance Festival of Free Latvians; Book 2: Out of the Ruins of Germany; Book 3: The Long Road Home. Bloomington, Indiana: Xlibris, 2015/2016.

—. *Kitty's Water Mill.* Translation of *Kaķīša Dzirnavas* by Kārlis Skalbe. Illustrations: Art Smith. Grand Rapids, Michigan: AKA Publishers International, 1986. Reissued with illustrations by Ināra Garklāva, Animated Film Studio Dauka, Riga: Zvaiggzne ABC, 1996.

—. *Latvian Folk Tales. Riga:* Zvaiggzne ABC, 1998. Includes twenty-eight folk tales in English translations.

Bibliography

Ancelāne, Alma, ed. with introduction. *Latviešu tautas teikas* (Latvian historical folk legends.) Riga: Zinātne, 1988.

Dobelis, Eduards, ed. *Aspazijas Drāma*, vol. I. Waverly, Iowa: Latvju Grāmata, 1963.

Freibergs, Vaira Vīķis and Imants Freibers. *Saules Dainas* (*Latvian Sun Songs*), illustrated by Inese Jansons. Montreal: Helios, 1988.

Laime, Sandis. *Nakts Raganas* (*Witches of the Night*): Riga: LU literatūras, fokloras un mākslas institūts (Latvia University literature, folklore and art institute), 2013.

Latkovski, Leonard Sr., "Wizards and Witches in Latvian Folklore." Lecture delivered at the Seventh Conference on Baltic Studies, Georgetown University, Washington DC, June 1980.

Tatar, Maria, ed. introduction by A. S. Byatt. *The Annotated Brothers Grimm*. New York: W. W. Norton & Co., 2004.

Traxler, Hans. Photographer Peter V. Tresckow. *Die Wahrheit über Hänsel und Gretel* Reinbeck at Hamburg: Rowohlt, 1983.

Untermeyer, Louis and Bryna, ed., illustrated by Lucille Corcos. New York: The Heritage Press, 1962.

***

Latvijas pērles (*Pearls of Latvia*). Twenty-two postcards of the most beautiful castles, palaces, and manors in Latvia. Riga: AGB, n.d.
Google: *Witch hunts in Livonia.* Also: *The Truth about Hansel and Gretel.*

***

Interviews with members of Latvia University folklore researchers about witch/wizard hunts and trials in Livonia during the Dark Ages. Riga: 1990.

Radio lecture heard in Berlin, December 1990, about the origin of elves.

Testimony of the granddaughter of a servant subjected to her barons' *first rights.*

ENDNOTES

1 Hans Traxler, *Die Wahrheit über Häsel und Gretel,* Hamburg, Germany: Rowohlt, 1983, 73-74.

2 Traxler, 74.

3 Traxler, 76–79.

4 Leonard Latkovski Sr., "Wizards and Witches in Latvian Folklore," lecture delivered at the seventh conference on Baltic Studies, Georgetown University, Washington DC, June 1980.

5. The truth of Traxler's book has been challenged. Google *Die Wahrheit über Hänsel und Gretel.*